I0614992

Harry Furniss

Royal Academy Antics

Harry Furniss

Royal Academy Antics

ISBN/EAN: 9783742819833

Manufactured in Europe, USA, Canada, Australia, Japa

Cover: Foto ©Andreas Hilbeck / pixelio.de

Manufactured and distributed by brebook publishing software
(www.brebook.com)

Harry Furniss

Royal Academy Antics

BY

HARRY FURNISS.

CASSELL & COMPANY, LIMITED:
LONDON, PARIS & MELBOURNE.
1890.

CONTENTS.

———•◦•———

viii   *Contents.*

PREFACE.

My object in producing this little volume is to point out, as briefly and pleasantly as possible, the necessity of a truly National Academy of Art in England.

In doing this it is possible that I may make the Royal Academy appear ridiculous. If I fail, I may bring ridicule upon myself. I ask, before you decide between us, to read this book from cover to cover

HARRY FURNISS.

London, May, 1890.

BEFORE ELECTION.   AFTER ELECTION.

TO THE YOUNGER MEMBERS OF

THE ROYAL ACADEMY,

TO WHICH THE ABOVE SKETCH REFERS,

I RECOMMEND THIS BOOK ;

TO ALL OUTSIDERS, WHO, LIKE MYSELF, DISLIKE HUMBUG,

I INSCRIBE IT.

ROYAL ACADEMY ANTICS.

Preliminary Antics.

CHARLES I. founded the first Academy under the name of the Museum Minervæ (1636), which was held at the house of Lord Francis Kynaston, in Covent Garden. This institution was not for the cultivation of painting, sculpture, and architecture alone, but embraced science, mathematics, foreign languages, riding, fortification, antiquities, and the science of medals. This truly comprehensive Academy shared the fate of the rest of Charles's projects, good and bad, for some uncivil people made themselves troublesome, and the result was a civil war, in which, as usual, the weakest went to the wall, thence to Whitehall, where an operation was

B

performed which proved fatal. The next we hear of Academies is that John Evelyn of Wootton formed a very good scheme for such an institution. Knowing the man he was, this seems very probable, but that it never got beyond the scheme stage is equally characteristic of this amiable dreamer.

Sir Godfrey Kneller had the next try in 1711, but the affair was only a squabbling shop, and being but weak, was killed one day by a caricature. Hogarth says that "the President and his adherents found themselves comically represented marching in ridiculous procession round the walls of the room ; the proprietors put a padlock on the door, and the subscribers did the same "—a very convenient door to have accommodation for so many padlocks. Sir James Thornhill was at the head of one of the petty factions who assisted to ring the knell of this last concern, and he forthwith started another Academy in his back garden, and gave away tickets ; but he was too English for Covent Garden, and no one went, so he banged the door, but found a padlock unnecessary, as there was no one to keep out.

Mr. Vanderbank, after having been a thorn in the side of this last President, consummated his rebellion by starting a new show in an old meeting-house. But even his attractive foreign name failed to draw subscribers, so he bethought himself of a shocking "artful dodge ;" he introduced, and advertised as a special attraction, a female model, "to make it more inviting," says Hogarth. A year or two sufficed to see the end of this peep-show, for an unfeeling landlord, not receiving his rent, distrained upon the stove, lamp, scrubbing-brush, and floorcloth, and the model too.

In 1734 Hogarth thought that he had a nucleus for a new Academy too good to be wasted, for he possessed what he calls Sir James Thornhill's "neglected apparatus." Therefore he started the apparatus, and it worked so well that for thirty years the St. Martin's Lane meteor was visible in the sky of art.

Whilst this luminary was pursuing its steady and undeviating course, another celestial phenomenon appeared, for the

Dilettante Society resolved upon a mighty antic which resulted in a sort of Aurora Borealis. From 1849 to 1853 they were maturing a scheme which culminated in a resolution to buy some land in Cavendish Square and build there a fane for Art upon the plan of the temple at Pola, but it ended in a frost. Apparently the Society of Arts wanted to keep all the illuminating business in their own hands, so they snuffed out the new concern.

The history of Hogarth's St. Martin's Lane institution now becomes the history of Art in England. In the midst of its career occurred the birth of British Art, the foundling.

In 1739 Captain Coram built a hospital for little waifs, and it was here, through an ingenious antic of William Hogarth, that John Bull came across his own neglected artistic baby. First Hogarth painted his famous portrait of the founder (which I have here parodied). Then when the first wing of the building

JOHN BULL DISCOVERING THE FOUNDLING, BRITISH ART.
(*After Hogarth.*)

was finished in 1745, he and eighteen other artists agreed to adorn its walls with paintings, and to meet annually on Nov. 5th to drink claret and punch in honour of the landing of William III.

It must appear that from the very first the Foundling Hospital was largely used by a class for whom it was certainly not originally intended, for it appears to have been a fashionable lounge in these early days; consequently the little picture antic took very well, for many of the aristocracy who would never have gone out of their way to see the pictures, saw them here, and it was the success of this first appearance in public which led to the artists determining to hold an annual exhibition of their works elsewhere. In their resolution, however, they did not confine themselves to paintings for the classes proposed to be included were painters, sculptors, architects, engravers, chasers, seal-cutters, and medallists.

It is important to note that although these gentlemen resolved to make a charge for admission to their annual show, they did not resolve to pocket the proceeds, but to raise money to distribute among " those artists whose age, infirmities, or other lawful hindrances prevent them from being any longer can-didates for fame "—a nice, graceful way of putting it, much prettier than the brutal " Relief of distressed and decayed brethren " of a rather later date.

The first annual exhibition was held in the rooms of the Society of Arts on 21st April, 1760, and closed 8th May, and during that time 6,582 sixpenny catalogues were sold—the Society of Arts refused to let them charge for admission. The chief antic which marked this show was that the Society of Arts insisted on exhibiting among the pictures of these accomplished painters the drawings of their art school students, and vastly misled the public by labelling them " First Prize," &c., which of course caused the innocent British Public to crowd around these youthful efforts, wondering where the signs of genius were which gave them pre-eminence over these paintings which they would have considered much better.

In 1761 the Society again applied for the use of the rooms

of the Society of Arts, proposing to stipulate that every one visiting the exhibition must buy a shilling catalogue as a ticket of admission. This the Society of Arts refused to sanction, so the majority of the artists took a room in Spring Gardens, and there was held their second exhibition. The catalogue was em- bellished with a frontispiece and tail-piece from Hogarth's pencil —and a vignette by Wall; thirteen thousand copies of this cata- logue were sold, realising £650. The minority who chose to secede from the Society held an exhibition in the rooms of the Society of Arts, and styled themselves " A free Society of Artists associated for the relief of the distressed and decayed brethren," &c. &c. It is not clear how the unfortunate " decayed " could greatly benefit by the efforts of a Society whose sole source of income was the sale of sixpenny catalogues, nor does it appear in what manner the Lying-in Hospital, the Middlesex Hospital, or the Asylum for Female Orphans can be made to come under the head of " distressed and decayed brethren "—and their first earnings went to these charities in two at least of which they could hardly hope to reach the brethren.

This Society for the propagation of decay soon found affairs ripe for a change, and the time came for them to gather in a harvest of shillings ; in 1765 they cut the Society of Arts, and to show they were a " Free Society," took a furniture store in Covent Garden for their next show.

They now relinquished their attentions to the Female Orphans and others, and turned the concern into a kind of lodge for the benefit chiefly of their own members when sick. Then they were stricken with the Academy itch ; but it was a sup- pressed form of the disease, occurring in the unfortunate year of the epidemic (1768), and they succumbed to an over-dose of West's Penny Royal, the noted Yankee quack nostrum.

Meanwhile the principal body prospered, and in 1765 secured a Royal Charter, and thenceforth was known as the " Incor- porated Society of Artists of Great Britain." And then the rows commenced. The indefiniteness of the terms of the charter was probably intentional on the part of the scheming Directo.s,

and allowed all kinds of antics, which bred a chronic turbulence.
The cap was put on their folly by their treasurer Dalton, who
had lately started a print shop in Pall Mall, and failed, so he
thought it his duty to the Society to let them the place for an -
academy. He successfully earwigged the King (whose librarian
he had been) to make one of his charming declarations about
taking Art under his wing ("poor thing!"), and the only thing
remaining to do was to erase the words "Print Warehouse," and
write up "Royal Academy," and the thing was done. Next
came the question of "chattels"—lamps, stove, busts, &c.; a
happy thought was to swoop down on St. Martin's Lane. To
effect this coup, Dalton and Moser vamped up a bogus declara-
tion, which deluded the "Fellows" with the idea that they would
be benefited by handing over their little all, and the "sticks"
went over to Pall Mall, and when the fledglings presented
themselves at the new nest they had to pay a guinea, and found
a lot of strange birds of every profession—or none—on an equal
footing with themselves, made free of the place for no earnest
purpose, by the simple payment of the guinea fee.

War now commenced between "Fellows" and "Directors,"
the former being in a large majority, the latter being in power,
and meaning to keep so by hook or crook, and refusing to
introduce any improvements suggested by the other men—
mean fellows. But the "fellahs" carried the day, turned out
sixteen Directors, and President and Treasurer, appointing
Joshua Kirby in place of Francis Hayman as President. This
party, headed by Chambers, West, Cotes, and Moser, at once
combined to start a new Academy (1768), and petitioned
George III. successfully. In this they declare their intentions
limited to the cultivation of painting, sculpture, and architecture,
and maintenance of a school of design. They modestly say
they expect to be able to pay their way, but ask that in exchange
for a little flattery, the King will pay any deficiency, and so keep
them afloat on the raft of royal favour and munificence, while
the parent and rival societies sink or swim by their own efforts
alone.

THE FOUR CONSPIRATORS

Royal Academy Antics.

" A Royal patron on the sly secured,
Which from the first its cheek to shame inured. *

THE antics of the Royal Academy would fill many volumes. A
royal antic founded it. George III., who had no knowledge of
Art, thought he would do something to give himself an air of
"culchaw." He saw nothing in Reynolds, preferred West's
works because they were "smoother," and Dance's because they
were "cheaper." And in West the King found a 'cute Yankee,
who wheedled him into a mock interest in the artists' quarrels of
the period (which I have outlined in the preceding chapter), and
" piled it on" until he hailed him as " Patron of the Arts," and
so, fooled "to the top of his bent," George fell in with West's
self-interested scheme with the gusto of a born conspirator.

"'Mum's the word,'" said the King ; "we'll bowl over the
Incorporated Society and the Free Society. Work it, West.
I'll have the *kudos*, you painter chaps the coin. Yankee-doodle
can see my people are ruled by snobbery, eh? and 'Royal' to
any art show will shut up the people's free and enlightened
exhibitions pretty quick."

* Soden's " Rap at the R.A."

West rushed off to tell the news to Chambers, Moser, and Cotes. The four conspirators formed themselves into a committee to draw up a plan of the Royal Academy,* and the strictest secrecy was observed, West running to-and-fro between his co-plotters and the King.†

Antic the First.

THE story of the triumph of trickery is pretty well known ; the little drama at Windsor provides the key to all the after-history of the Royal Academy. The poet has sung of quite another tyranny that "Freedom shrieked when Kosciusko fell"—for Kosciusko read Kirby, and the line will be true of modern British Art.

West was at Windsor Castle showing to the King and Queen his picture of "The Departure of Regulus for Rome," which was his first commission from royalty, when Joshua Kirby, the President of the Incorporated Society, was announced. The King consulted with his consort in German, and Mr. Kirby was admitted. The painters, it seems, did not know each other, and the King introduced Mr. Kirby to his American protégé. Kirby politely joined in the general praise of the picture, and turning to West expressed his hope that it would be shown at the Society's coming exhibition. The painter, turning to King Catspaw, says that the matter rests with His Majesty.

"Assuredly," replied royalty ; "I shall be happy to let the work be shown to the public."

"Then, Mr. West, you will send it to my exhibition ?" added the President of the Incorporated Society.

---

* See Salt's "Life of West," and Carey's "Observations on the Probable Decline or Extinction of British Historical Painting."
† Edwards' "Anecdotes of Painters."

" No," His Majesty interposed ; " it must go to *my* exhibition, to the *Royal Academy.*"

Mr. Kirby was thunderstruck, the battery was unmasked. Astonished and humiliated, the worthy man retired from the

A BLACK SPOT IN THE HISTORY OF ENGLISH ART.

royal presence, leaving his rival master of the situation. The unmerited blow was a severe one, and whether it hastened his end or not, it is certain that the few remaining years of his life were greatly embittered by the results of his enemy's unscrupulous treachery. Concerning Mr. Kirby in this connection, I quote from an excellent article in *Once a Week*, by Mr. Dutton Cook (one of the most graceful as well as the most straightforward of modern writers) : " He had risen from quite humble life to a position of some eminence entirely by his own exertions. It was admitted that he had attained the position of President of the Incorporated Society without intrigue on his own part, and that both by reason of his professional skill and his private worth, he was entitled to the respect alike of the friends and foes of that institution. The King condescended to play an ignoble part when he took pains to mortify and distress so honest a gentleman. Rival artists might conspire against a society from which they had seceded, and seek to mine its position; but His Majesty stooped very low when he lent his royal hand to fire the train. However, he had thrown himself heart and soul into the project for founding a new society—the Royal Academy. So that he reared that edifice he seemed to care little how he sullied his fingers in the process." I quote this to show that the intrigue had not even the excuse of crushing out a discredited or unworthy faction, but that, on the contrary, it was a contemptible pandering to unblushing and self-interested sycophancy, involving practically the ruin of all that the best spirits in the art world had laboured for since the commencement of the century, and the substitution of a very "house built upon the sand" of unmitigated selfishness and treachery.

Antic the Second.—Body-Snatching.

PENNY WISE.

ON the day following the event at Windsor, the nobodies who saw their chance of getting a slice of the Royal Academy cake met at the house of one of them—Wilton, a sculptor (who was given the secretaryship), to nominate the office-bearers. They appointed Chambers, treasurer; Moser, keeper; Penny, professor of painting; and Dr. Hunter, professor of anatomy.

Chambers was an architect, and among his pickings was the rebuilding of Somerset House. He was a knight of the Swedish order, whether for writing his "Dissertation on Oriental Gardening" (and the Cultivation of Swedes?), I cannot say. Suffice it to relate that, in spite of Walpole and the poet Mason, Chambers, being an original member of the Royal Academy, was sheltered under the royal wing, and long continued to build chambers and churches to delight the world and load his coffers ; the poet Mason perforce yielding him the supremacy of the trowel, whilst Walpole reached the top of the architectural fabric.

It was not difficult to assign these minor offices, but the tough piece in the jobbery fire was left, as usual, to the last. The council of crawlers knew very well that, however easy it is to bamboozle a king with judicious flattery, the public must be dealt with more cautiously. They well knew the public would not stand West as President, and astutely selected Mr. Reynolds for the office. Now Reynolds had been kept completely in the dark as to their plots, and, further, he had previously expressed himself very plainly that he would have nothing at all to do with them, as he considered they were endeavouring to "raise a schism in the arts," and to do him justice art was more to Reynolds than place or plunder. Mr. Reynolds had therefore to be bought over, so the conspirators sent him a Penny,* but he was not to be had so cheap ; " No, not for a Sovereign!" cried Reynolds, in a voice that nearly stopped the circulation of the copper currency, and poor Penny turned tail, and went back to the schism-shop for change. Things now became serious, so the Council resolved to resort to body-snatching. Hastily planning an effective "wake" when the "mummy" should arrive, West took a coach to Reynolds's house.

The Yankee bounded upstairs, and into the presence of the great Joshua, who looked up, mildly surprised, through his huge spectacles, and was about to utter a remonstrance, when brother Ben broke in—

* Edward Penny ("Twopence" ought to have been his name—"Penny plain, Twopence coloured"), Professor of Painting. The lectures he delivered in this office he promised to publish—in penny numbers presumably—but they never appeared.

"Didn't take Penny, eh, stranger? guess Penny's a hooter, an' that's three parts of a durned fool, eh? You know my chum, George? eh? Not much? fool? wall that's so, you bet, but I reckon that hoss knows when I'm behind him and gets right through. Wall, as I was sayin', he sez to me, 'Don't be a fool, West, boss the durned show yourself and I'll make you a knight right off,' but I jest put *my* hand upon *my* heart and said something in Latten, I don't recollect which, but His Most Gracious wunk an said 'that's so,' and 'there's a knighthood a-begging, Reynolds will have it!'" *

The Yankee walked to the window and looked out. "I reckon, Sir Joshua, you'd be better for a drive, and we can talk as we go along." The great painter consented, and the Angel of Art gave a little shudder.

Alas, Mr. Reynolds! all is vanity! Had you stood out against this conspiracy to monopolise freedom in art, we might have been to-day advanced instead of having an art history whose chief progress has been in a backward direction! For a mushroom title you gave a head to a worthless body with a fishy corporation, which monopolising monster has, by a snobbish and ignorant following, crushed free art and action under this Juggernaut of a "Royal Instrument." True, you apologised by saying that you knew it gave additional splendour to your works in vulgar eyes.† Nowadays you would have demanded a baronetcy or peerage for the same reason—pictures are dearer, titles are cheaper.

SIR JOSHUA'S PRICES RISE.

To return to the conspirators. Like a band of "Moon-

---

lighters," the members of this clique were anxiously awaiting
the return of their chief kidnapper; their theatrical effect was
all rehearsed, and they impatient to let it off. After two hours
waiting, West drove up to the door with his prey, and was in
their midst, accompanied by the bewildered Reynolds. In-
stantly the whole company leaped to their feet, crying out—
" President ! President !"* Mr. Reynolds seemed much affected
at the compliment, but asked for time to consult his friends,
Dr. Johnson and Mr. Burke. This greatly disappointed the
clique, anxious as boys to have their new toy, the " Royal Instrument," and flourish it aggressively in the faces of the other
boys. Vest and Coats—I mean West and Cotes—certain of
the success of this " try-on " with Reynolds, expected to wait on
the King with the suit complete on the following morning ; but
Reynolds, Johnson, and Burke took a fortnight † to swallow this
"intrigue of the very basest kind." Surely, had all been fair and
honourable, three such men would not have hesitated so long.

The Royal Academy of England.

I GIVE my authority for all I have stated. It is easily seen that
the Royal Academy was founded in what we call an un-English
—*i.e.*, an underhand—way ; but the constitution of the Royal
Academy, be it remarked, was the handiwork of foreigners. Its
very foundation is un-English, since, of its four originators, only
one was an Englishman, thus :—West (American), Chambers
(Swedish), Moser (Swiss), Cotes (English). Small wonder then
that nearly a third of the original members were foreigners,
whilst many of the best painters of the day were not members,
as they had the hardihood to continue members of reputable
societies, and as such could not be received into this truly
national institution.

* Sandby's " History of the Royal Academy." † Northcote.

The "Instrument Antic."

WE have seen how this interesting contrivance was delayed in its completion by the hesitation and want of sympathy of Mr. Reynolds. It may be instructive to take a glance at the document which was, and is, the sole charter of our Royal Academy. When the four conspirators made their appeal to George III., His Majesty asked them to draw up their plans in writing. The four plotter birds retired to their rookery to consult, and when they had cawed the matter over, up got the Yankee bird and croaked—

> " Who'll write the Instrument ? "
> " I," said the Swede ;
> And they all cried " Agreed !
> You write the Instrument."

So the Scandinavian architect drew out a hurried plan, got " as many artists as the shortness of time would allow " * to sign it, and took it to the King, who wrote below, in questionable English, " I approve of this plan ; let it be put in execution," and appended the royal signature.

Such being the origin of the document constituting " The Royal Academy of Arts in London,"—of which the King of England declared himself " patron, protector, and supporter," we cannot marvel to find that it provides that the members shall not be " members of any other society of artists ; " that while it expressly excludes engravers (*English* engravers it ought to have specified) it names as a member Bartolozzi, who it is true was *not* an *English* engraver, and excludes Strange, Sharpe, and Woollett who were ; † that it nominates a Swiss goldchaser (Moser), a coach painter (John Baker), a sign painter (Samuel Wale), two women, both Swiss (the Misses Moser and Kauffmann), and a rabble of foreigners of all nations whose

---

* Dutton Cook.

† " Since Sir Robert Strange, and Woollett, and Sharpe were denied admission to the Academy it is quite certain that the art has suffered."—PYE.

names are happily forgotten and need not be recorded here. One touch of humour alone enlivens this otherwise dull document; when we consider the eminently lofty morality displayed by the projectors of the concern, it is amusing to find that they considered it necessary to stipulate that members must be "of high moral character."

Article VIII. of this Instrument provides that "The King is graciously pleased to pay all deficiencies;" and he actually did —during the first eleven years of the Academy—pay about £5,000 to their funds.

Before quitting this subject, I may append the fact that when George IV., seeing that this Instrument was an unsatisfactory foundation for a national institution, desired to incorporate the Royal Academy by charter, the body cleverly, but not ingenuously, declined; for they preferred to dispose of their increasing wealth in their own way, without acknowledging any responsibility or rendering any account to the nation.

It would be wearisome to follow the Royal Academy through the first hundred years of its existence; its antics have been many and various, and their history would require volumes to chronicle. My readers who have patiently followed me thus far may be consoled by the assurance that the briefest survey is all which I propose to take of the period from the foundation of the R.A. up to our own times.

The See=Saw Antic.

PERHAPS the most extraordinary fact in connection with this remarkable institution is the success with which its executive has contrived to maintain it in its conveniently anomalous position. I have already shown that the Academy positively declined a Royal Charter when it was desired to allow itself to become properly incorporated; this would not have suited the book of those most concerned at all, for their game was to hold fast to all the advantages they enjoyed as a public institution, whilst refusing to accept responsibility of any kind on the ground of being a private society.

This is how the see-saw works :— *

Says the Public to the President, " Pray, good sir, this is an excellent exhibition, and I am delighted to see so many silver shillings passing across your counters ; pray where may I find the proceedings of your ' Royal ' institution, and the records of your administration of the vast funds which evidently pass through your hands ? "

" Oh, my dear Public," says the President, gently inclining the see-saw so that the " No Responsibility " side ascends, " these things are not for us; we are a private concern, and a very paying concern, too, between you and me ; good thing! no opposition ! But we don't show our balance sheets ; why should we ? You wouldn't if you were a private concern, would you ? Of course not."

" Oh, thank you, sir, certainly, quite right. I was evidently under a misapprehension."

Next there comes an officious person who asks a question of Parliament. " Certain rooms in a public building are at present occupied by a society other than a government institution. I desire to be informed whether this Society pays any rent to the Exchequer, and if not, why not ? " After a due and proper delay for the re-adjustment of the see-saw, comes the reply, " The Council of the Royal Academy has satisfied the powers that be, that that institution is, strictly speaking, a public institution rendering great public service to the nation, and as such enjoys certain inalienable privileges, and holds its charter directly from the Crown." And the officious person subsides.

Could the Royal Academy be regarded purely as a private institution, then all objection to its proceedings would be deprived of its pertinence, for then might a dozen enterprising persons start a dozen Royal Academies, and we should in a

* *See* Frontispiece.

short time have five hundred capable painters rejoicing in the
suffix " R.A.," and the day of the National Academy would be
nigh. But, unfortunately for Art, George III. lived and reigned
a very long time ; and it is characteristic of this monarch that
whilst he made the most unconditional promises that all worthy
artistic societies should receive equal patronage from him, he
had no intention whatever of keeping his word, and the " show "
run by his favourite West received not only his almost exclusive
attention, but also his assistance in hard cash when the parent
and rival society was sinking neglected into oblivion. George
III. thus saw the Royal Academy so firmly established through
his favour and help that its monopoly has never since been
seriously threatened.

Early Trumpeting Antics.

I CANNOT pass by the proceedings which marked the opening
of the first exhibition of the Royal Academy, so very symbolic
are they of the modest attitude assumed·by the body throughout
its career.

On April 26th, 1769, a banquet was held at the St. Alban's
Tavern. At this function there were recited odes written for the
occasion, in which the singular absence of anything like " blow,"
or " blatherskite," or high-pitched, far-fetched blarney is so
remarkable, that I venture to offer a sample—most inadequate—
as a model of what these " tall " compositions should be.

> " With rapture the prophetic Muse
> Her country's opening glory views ;
> Already sees with wondering eyes
> Our Titians and our Guidos rise :
> Sees new Palladios grace th' historic page,
> And British Raphaels charm a future age.
>
> Meantime, ye sons of Art, your offspring bring
> To grace your patron and your king.

. . . .

Bid painting's magic pencil trace
The features of his darling race.

. . . .

Bid some majestic structure rise to view
Worthy him and worthy you "

(This is only the merest fraction of this one ode ; it is too long to be given *in extenso.*)

Another ode ran through many stanzas in the same strain as this :—

" 'Tis yours, O well selected band,
To watch where infant genius blows,
To rear the flower with fostering hand
And every latent sweet disclose,
That arts unrivalled long may reign
Where George protects the polished train."

This is not a bad beginning. Speaking of banquets nerves the wings of my historic muse to a flight of fifty years, and brings up the

----

Jubilee Gorge Antic.

IN 1818 the R.A.'s were much exercised to find a fitting way of celebrating the glorious occasion of their Jubilee. All were agreed that it must be commemorated by some "enduring memorial." Some suggested to produce an elaborate and magnificent history of the institution, but modesty prevailed, and they didn't. Others were in favour of striking a medal, but the idea fell flat. Then a brilliant idea struck someone—"A big blow-out!" The very thing! And thus was erected the "enduring memorial" of artistic jubilation. The odes, if any, on this occasion were not made so much of. The R.A. had long since learned that "good wine needs no bush," and that even bad wine is more elevating than middling verse ; so they ate and they drank, while the "prophetic Muse," with "wondering eyes," looked down upon her "Titians and her Guidos," her "Raphaels," and "new Palladios," and murmured, "WORTHY HIM AND WORTHY YOU!" till the President's wheel-barrow was announced.

Speaking of medals, too, reminds me of the

First Gold Medal Antic.

THERE was an indolent, pretentious young man who studied at the Academy schools, and consequently found out very soon that interest and favour was much more useful there than ability or industry. He seems to have been well known to Dr. Johnson, whose kindness was often more conspicuous than his discretion when he was solicited to use his influence in favour of any young duffer such as our friend the student, whose appropriate name was Lowe. Mr. Lowe carefully curried favour in high places, and as a result he gained the first gold medal. Now the unfortunate title of the competition subject was "Time discovering Truth." This subject must have been prompted by the "prophetic Muse," for Time did discover the truth in this case, and it was soon generally known that the gold medal had been awarded for the worst work to the student who had most indolence, incapacity, and personal interest among the judges; and so will Time discover the truth in every piece of jobbery the Academy is guilty of. Let them give the same subject for the next gold medal competition, and award the medal to the student who treats it as suggested on next page.

The Deluge Antic.

THIS same student was the hero also of another low proceeding on the part of the R.A., which I may here relate, though I shall have occasion to refer to it again. In 1783 the Council rejected

C 2

a picture of the Deluge. As soon as their determination was known, the painter—no other than our Mr. Lowe—got Dr. Johnson to write to Sir Joshua Reynolds and Sir James Barry, "to procure the revocation of this incapacitating edict"—which is Johnsonese for "Shut your eyes, and job it in, to oblige yours truly"—and the Council obligingly revoked, and "The Deluge" had a room to itself, where it excited the astonishment of all who saw it, for it was trash, pure and simple—a fitting monument to jobbery.

(Detail to be filled in by the student after he has read this volume.)

House-Moving Antics.

IN one matter the spirit of advance has certainly had a good time with the Royal Academy; that is, in the matter of housing. I have already stated that their first home was in Pall Mall, at the unsuccessful print shop. Here the first eleven exhibitions were held, namely 1769 to 1779 inclusive. Rooms in Somerset House had been set aside for the use of the Academy schools since 1771, and in 1780 the exhibitions commenced to be held there and continued until 1836. About the latter year there was a general feeling that the Royal Academy had grown out of the lodging provided for it by the nation, and in order to give better opportunity for the display of all the now very large amount of really good work sent in a fine suite of rooms was given to them in the National Gallery in Trafalgar Square.

This year of 1836 should have been a great year for the
Royal Academy, but it is difficult to speak with patience of the
Council's unfortunate success in defending the institution against
all suggestions of reform, and in disastrously defeating the party
that strove for the national good. A Royal Commission was
held to inquire into the working of the Royal Academy, and to
hear suggestions for its reformation ; but the reform party were
feebly championed, and the conservative crew tacked and
tacked about with each change of the wind, till the Commis-
sioners seem to have been deluded into the idea that if the
R.A. was not perfect, still reform was proceeding so rapidly
within its walls that no aid from them was required. The
whole thing consequently ended in a few futile suggestions
being offered, and things being left practically exactly as they
were before.

For twenty-seven years after their removal to Trafalgar
Square the Academy was free from any serious disturbance,
although a great deal of dissatisfaction was felt by many an able
artist who saw that, with the advantages the institution possessed,
much more ought to be done for Art.

In 1863, however, this feeling came to a head, and another
Royal Commission was the result.

The objectors were now stronger, and it was pretty clearly
shown that the Royal Academy was acting as a close corporation whose efforts were first and last all for the benefit and
aggrandisement of its few members, and that the general
interests of the nation's art were entirely subservient to the
commercial fortunes of these members ; and yet, *mirabile dictu !*
this Commission achieved as little as the former one. It is true
the Academy felt the pressure, and found it wise to box the
compass even more vigorously than before ; the great cry being
" We cannot do justice to all unless we have more room in
which to exhibit."

The suggestion being advanced to give to the R.A. the
mansion known as Burlington House, the Council cautiously
accepted the offer, promising that if they were granted that site

they would provide space for three times as many pictures as they had been able to show in Trafalgar Square, also that in future no picture should be accepted but not hung, and that every work hung should be fairly visible. How they made good this promise was well shown by Mr. T. J. Gullick, in his pamphlet, "The Royal Academy, the 'Outsiders,' and the Press," written in 1869—one year after the removal of the R.A. to their new palace in Piccadilly. After a careful examination of the catalogues he concludes, "There is (excluding the exceptional exhibition of Mr. Goodall's sketches) an increase in the number of oil paintings of *only six in all !* But of the whole number of oil paintings in the present exhibition not less than 167 are by Academicians and Associates—42 more than last year—and 70 by foreign artists— 60 more than last year"—consequently "there is a positive *reduction* of one hundred this year in the number of works by native outsiders."

Satire and invective falls feeble and unavailing beside the withering condemnation of these simple, straightforward facts. Well might struggling talent have risen at this juncture and flung the specious promises of the Council in their faces, with Byron's scathing words (used in a less honourable quarrel)—

> "This was the pledge you made to me,
> And here's exactly what it's worth."

And better still could they have carried the parallel further, and written the words (as the poet did) "on the back of the deed of separation."

But the R.A., like the cat of proverb, has nine lives, and the dissatisfaction fell as harmless and as useless as the rain upon the sound roof of their costly temple in Piccadilly.

Presidential Antics.

THE first, and probably the best, President the Academy ever had—Sir Joshua Reynolds—was not above antics of the very first water.

In 1790 Messrs.—or, rather, Signor and Monsieur—Bonomi and Fuseli were candidates for a vacancy in the ranks of the Royal Academicians. Now, there never was a doubt that Fuseli was vastly more worthy of the honour than his rival. This Reynolds admitted; but he had reasons for favouring the less worthy competitor, and he strove his hardest to force Bonomi's election. For all the President's efforts, Fuseli was elected by a majority of two to one, whereon Reynolds resigned the Presidency and renounced all connection with the Royal Academy.

The Royal Academy, however, sent a deputation to the great man, and succeeded in reconciling him, so that he continued in office till his death, two years later.

Another incident—though its chief actor was never President—may show that more than one celebrated man was ready in the early days to take a trumpery excuse for quitting the ranks of the Academicians. Thomas Gainsborough in 1784 sent a group of princesses, full length; and with the picture a letter demanding in peremptory terms that it should be hung on the line ; the penalty of disobedience being that his mightiness

would never again exhibit at the Academy—" and this I swear by God." And he did not. He died in 1788.

Benjamin West was the second President, and he began his antics at a very early age. His first effort in art was made at the age of seven, when he was set to rock the cradle while his

little sister slept ; and while so engaged, he was accidentally
struck by her smile, whereon he revengefully hit it off with a
stick dipped in red and black ink.   And the Chief of the
Cherokee Indians popped his head in.   "What, no paint ? "
And he gave him a pinch of yellow ochre out of his silver
snuff-box, and the infant plucked a bushel of camel's hair from
the cat's tail, and became President of the Royal Academy.

West and Reynolds each were afflicted by artistic jealousies,
but the weapons they used in the fight were very different, and
characteristic of the two men.   Reynolds never hid his enmity
for an instant towards those few whom he thought possible
rivals; and his determined antagonism to Romney was the cause
of the latter never exhibiting at the Royal Academy.   So violent was his dislike to his distinguished *confrère*, that, trumpery
as it may seem, Reynolds would never even mention Romney
by name, referring to him only as "the man in Cavendish
Square."   West's behaviour, on the other hand, savours much
more of the man of the world, and justly met with severe blame.
In 1793--the year following his election—his friend, the Rev.
Bromley brought out, under West's eye, a " History of the Fine
Arts," in which West was held up to praise to the detriment
of Sir Joshua Reynolds (deceased) and Fuseli (then living), the
latter being opposed to the President.   This publication raised

a storm of indignation, and the second volume never saw day-light.

During the life of George III. West kept in high favour with the King, and received many commissions at extravagant prices. When, in 1801, the King was " afflicted," art matters in the royal household fell into the hands of Wyatt, the royal architect. This gentleman was not a fool, and had the courage of his opinions, so he ordered West to stop his supply of daubs. George, however, got well, and West complained to him ; whereon the King said, "Go on, West ; I'll look after you!" which he did, to the tune of £1,000 a-year. West received, on the whole, over £34,000 from George III., for work which would not now fetch 34,000 shillings.

There seems some fitness in the fact that the deaths of both painter and patron occurred within three months of each other.

West's vanity is very funnily illustrated by the following story:—He was on a visit to Paris, and certainly seems to have been very well received, concerning which he wrote, "Wherever I went men looked at me. . . . I was one day at the Louvre, all eyes were upon me; and I could not help observing to Charles Fox, who happened to be walking with me, how strong was the love of art and admiration of its professors in France."

On his return from France, West found himself very unpopular, and sent in his resignation to the Council couched in such terms as to prove conclusively that the Council would be doing a very bad thing if they accepted it ; but the Council took him at his word, and for some months his old enemy Wyatt occupied the Presidential chair, till in the following year (1804) he was reinstated. Previous to this, however, West had been guilty of an antic which is unaccountable. Having exhibited his picture, "Hagar and Ishmael," in 1776, he sent it in again in 1803, but the Council happened to "schmell" a rat, and the picture had to be withdrawn. But this was not effected without some very severe remarks appearing in the newspapers.

West was succeeded in the Presidential Chair by Sir Thomas Lawrence—the high priest of the "curtain and column" school in portraiture. In his young days Lawrence was remarkable for his gift of pleasing, and this was his best friend through life. He was handsome and undoubtedly clever, and coming to London at an early age he was so successful in attracting notice in high places, that at the age of twenty-one the King insisted on the Academy electing him an Associate against their rules, which lay down the minimum age as twenty-four. His first antic was to exhibit ten portraits in his first year (1792) ; and although he did not get up to this record again, he usually showed eight portraits every year during the thirty-eight years he was exhibiting at the Royal Academy. Flattery was Lawrence's stock-in-trade, for though he was an excellent painter he would certainly never have been so extraordinarily popular and fashionable had he not persistently flattered his sitters in a way that would not be tolerated now. The poet Campbell very happily says of his portraits that the sitters " Seem to have got into a drawing-room in the mansions of the blessed, and to be looking at themselves in the mirrors." Opie equally truly says that " He made coxcombs of his sitters, and allowed them to make a coxcomb of

him." The latter would be difficult, for we hear that at the age of seventeen he pleased himself so well that he offered to stake his reputation against any painter living (a safe stake). There is, unfortunately, little doubt that he was an inveterate flirt and ladykiller ; his portraits of Mrs. Siddons were doubtless valuable, but her daughter's honour was too high a price to pay for them ; and when he undertook to paint the portrait of the Princess of Wales, it seems a pity that his zeal in the conscientious study of his royal model should have carried him so far into the privacy of the lady's apartments as to make the subject of a " Delicate Investigation," and a world-wide scandal. The world was also a loser through the great man's levities for he could not paint men, though his portraits of women were mostly admirable, and for seven years after this scandal his lady sitters fell off, so that he painted scarcely any but male portraits ; besides, the Regent naturally did not favour him so highly as did his merry spouse. Still, royal favour returned to him when the Regent became George IV., and that monarch had succumbed to the arch flatterer so far as to personally place a gold chain and medal around his neck on his election to the Presidency. Was this the reward for conformance to the rule already quoted which insists on men " of high moral character ? "*

SAINT LAWRENCE.
Design for a stained glass window to be placed in the Chapel of the Royal Academy.

Lawrence, like all young men without a spark of imagination, thought his forte was in huge and heroic imaginative works. In his early Academy days he tried "Satan Calling upon his Legions," which was a fiasco. " Pasquin " wickedly likened Belial to "a mad sugar-baker dancing naked in the conflagration of his own treacle." Fuseli accused Lawrence of stealing the idea from him, to which the portrait-painter's ready, but not too convincing, retort was that he certainly had taken Fuseli as his model, but had copied his person, not his work. " Prospero Raising the Wind " was another ill-fated and funnily-named effort in the ridiculous sublime ; some wag said it was designed to decorate

* Geo. H. Harlowe was a pupil of Lawrence's, but was refused admission to the Academy schools as a student, and later on refused as an Associate. Sandby says, " Foreign academies admitted him to their honours, but he could not with propriety have taken a place among the members of our Royal Academy, who are required by the Instrument to be men of fair moral character as well as artists of distinction."

So the R A. is a *moral Palladium* as well as a Temple of Art !

the Stock Exchange. Lawrence thought "Satan" his best
work, and at one time wrote to Mrs. Boucherette, "I am
very glad you like my 'Hamlet,' which, except my 'Satan,'
I think my best work." Anyhow, it seems to have bewitched
the R.A., and Satan has "got them in his eye" to this day, for
he hangs in their chamber of horrors.

Lawrence did one bad thing for portrait painters; he taught
them the vice of introducing two horizons in one picture. It
was not he, but one of his eminent disciples, who, having
painted a portrait of the Duke of Devonshire showing Chatsworth in the distance, was told that the drawing was all false
and impossible, and profoundly responded—"Yes, but you know
Chatsworth is on a devil of a hill."

Lawrence was so fond of royal patronage that when he received the freedom of his native city (Bristol), he could only call
it "the very highest honour that could have rewarded my professional labours—the protection of Majesty excepted." The
"protection" of George IV. the highest—"the very highest"—
honour! Strange and significant that this sycophant, as well as
his predecessor, died within a few months of his royal master
(1830).

Lawrence was always a spendthrift and always in debt; but
it is only fair to record that he seems to have been ever ready to
give wherever his aid was asked. It is further due to his
memory to quote his last words to the Royal Academy—and
had he lived for this alone the R.A. should thank him. "I am
now," said he, "advanced in life, and the time of decay is
coming; but come when it will, I hope to have the good sense
not to prolong the contest for fame with younger, and perhaps
abler, men. No self-love shall prevent me from retiring, and
that cheerfully, to privacy; and I consider that I shall but do
an act of justice to others, as well as mercy to myself."

These words should be writ large all over the walls of the
Royal Academy. Death prevented the resolution being put
to the test, for within a very short time the President was no
more.

SHEE.—WHO MUST BE OBEYED.

HE next President seems to have been selected for his negative qualities, for Sir Martin Archer Shee was neither a painter of much merit, nor a man of money, nor, like his predecessor, a society masher. Still, he wrote a tragedy, which the Lord Chamberlain (or his representative of those days) refused to license, certain "Rhymes on Art," which the public refused to read, and a novel not worth damning; and moreover Byron mentioned him in "English Bards and Scotch Reviewers," and surely these were qualifications enough for the President of the Royal Academy of England!

Shee came from the Emerald Isle to London full of hope, and thought to take the place by storm. He did not get his first pictures accepted by the R.A. He too soon learned the lesson that it is not by merit that a young man gets into the R.A., so he went to Burke, who went to Reynolds, and the next year (1791) his pictures were hung. Once again incapacity launched out into big canvases and fancy subjects; he also tried our old friend Prospero, but failed to "raise the wind." "Jephtha's Daughter" also helped him to waste his time, and then he sunk into weak portrait painting and poverty, and so was elected to the Presidency and £300 a year (1830), and died in 1850, at the age of eighty-one.

Sir Charles Lock Eastlake was President from 1850 to 1865. He can scarcely be credited with any antics worth the name; he also was more of a writer than a painter, but he abjured the poetic Muse, and chiefly devoted himself to the exposition of the dry theory and history of art. As far as painting is concerned, he started, like all the rest, on subjects. "Jairus' Daughter" was

his first love; then he went
to the land of macaroni
and gave the world some
middling landscapes. Later
he took to historical and
Scriptural subjects, which
were neither many nor ex-
cellent. Eastlake held many
official positions—such as
Secretary to the Commis-
sion for Decorating the
Houses of Parliament, Li-
brarian to the R.A., Keeper
of the National Gallery,
incurring in the latter some
very severe censure. After
his election as President,

A PAPER PRESIDENT.

he appears to have been chiefly employed as buyer for the
National Gallery. In one way this was a model President; he
not only did not occupy his full space in the Academy, but he
ceased to exhibit at all in 1855.

On Eastlake's death in 1865, Sir Edwin Landseer was
elected President, but
declined the office, after
really being President for
nine days. In fact, the
position was unpopular
apparently, for Maclise
also refused the job, and
Francis Grant was pressed
into the service. From
1866 to 1878 the President
seems to have got on very
well. He was another
respectable duffer; was
meant for the Bar, but

DIGNITY AND IMPUDENCE.

D

took to portrait painting, and became fashionable for want of a better.   Sir Francis Grant dying, he was succeeded (1878) by Frederick Leighton, the present President.

THE PRESENT FIGURE-HEAD.

Sir Frederick Leighton is acknowledged by all to be a model President of the Royal Academy. But, as Batty Todd says in *The Middleman*, "Figure-heads ain't much use in the navigation of the ship," and during the twelve years he has been its figure-head the Royal Academy ship has hardly deviated from the old, old course. Sir Frederick is handsome, learned, and courteous; he requires to do one thing to become strong, and that is——

But I have no wish to be personal. Indeed, I desire to state most emphatically that much as I object to the Royal Academy ship as a whole, I have always found the crew—when out of it—the best of fellows, and among them I have some old and valued friends.

Antics at School.

I VENTURE to say we all regret we were not more attentive at school, but this is after we forget how dry school was.   Fortunately common sense has reached us from Germany, and our little ones are taught in the Kindergarten in a way to attract and amuse them.   They swallow the pill of knowledge with the silver on, in place of being dosed with dry powder which revolts them.

Now why do we not make the introduction of Art more attractive to the boy? He is introduced to the School of Art as he is to the dentist, with this exception, the knowledge that he is about to draw with a stump, instead of having one drawn.

A cold, meaningless scroll is first placed in front of him, before which he sits and yawns, and tries to copy.

Then a cone is given to him, a ball, a triangle, anything, in fact, that is uninteresting, and he is kept copying them until he is tired. Next a head, a hand, or a foot is his fare, a sort of mutilated corpse in plaster of Paris, and about as cheering, to be stippled, crosshatched, and worked up for months.

By that time he sees the Art student's life is not a happy one ; he finds relief in throwing lumps of bread at the heads of other students, and a little extra excitement when he hits his professor by mistake.

Why not abolish this cold initiation, begin by giving the boy something to interest him, not to depress him ? We might then have more original artists.

There is no doubt that the chrysalis state of the artist is longer than that of other professions.

Mr. Frith, in his interesting autobiography lately published, remarks :—" Artists are slow to develop, showing clearly the severe technique that only patient years of study can overcome. The usual work of the boy artist is little or no criterion to their future chances. Consider the quality of mind and body requisite for a successful artistic career—long and severe study from antique statues from five to eight hours every day ; then many months' hard work from the life, with attendance at lectures, study of perspective, anatomy, etc. ; general reading to be attended to also—all this before painting is attempted, and when attempted the student may find he has no eye for colour ; I do not mean colour-blind, which is, of course, fatal, but that he is not appreciative of all the subtle tints and tones of flesh ; or what is more fearful still, he may find that he has all the

D 2

language of Art at his fingers' ends, and that he has nothing to say."

Nothing to say! This simply means that the student has no *originality*, no *ideas*, no *invention*.

Why, my principal object in parodying the Royal Academy lately, and in leaving my easel for the platform now, is to point out the conventionality, the poverty of invention, characteristic of our Art, and encouraged by our system of Art training. I quite agree with Mr. Seymour Haden, whose remark on this point is as sharp as his etching needle. He says:—

" I attach no value to technical education, or what tradition teaches.

" Too minute a rendering in matters of Art is bad ; such a process means an extension of the work over long passages of time, which must tend to weaken the primary ideas and conceptions of the artist. The great masters knew this and worked rapidly, knowing full well that if the sacred fire once languished it could not be re-illumined."

I will not weary you by recording the many alleged defects of the Academy schools.* One illustration will suffice to show you how absurd the system is.

The members of the Academy visit the school paid to teach

* Here are a few interesting mems. about the schooling of some artists :—
Martin was a pupil of Musso. Flaxman studied with his father, and at the Duke of Richmond's Gallery. He studied, indeed, a short time at the Academy, where he was refused the gold medal. Chantrey learned carving at Sheffield. Gibson was a ship carver at Liverpool. When Sir Thomas Lawrence became a probationer for admission to the schools of the Academy his claims were not allowed. The Academy taught, not Bonnington. No ; nor Danby, nor Stanfield. Dr. Munro directed the taste of Turner.— See *New Monthly Magazine*, May, 1833.
" It is sufficient to state that the Royal Academy was intended for the encouragement of historical paintings, that it is filled with landscapes and portraits ; that it was intended to incorporate and cheer on all distinguished students, that it has excluded and persecuted many of the greatest we possess ; and that at this moment, sixty-five years after its establishment, our greatest living artists, with scarcely any exception, have *not* been educated at an Academy intended, of course, *to* educate genius even more than to support it afterwards."—From " England and the English," Lord Lytton.

the young idea how to paint. Each artist enforces his own particular method and theory which upsets those of all the others, and all he does is to leave the student hopelessly bewildered. Fancy being taught to shave by different professors of the art !

One might tell you to shave up, another to shave down, another with a circular stroke, a fourth with a continuous long sweep from ear to ear.

Why, in the end you would cut your throat. And is not this patchwork Art-teaching suicidal to a student's progress ?

They manage these things better in France. There a student chooses his master, and works under his colours, and in his style.

He has the one master's method to study, and pulling his stroke his tuition travels faster, and when he paddles his own canoe he is not worried by conflicting currents of thought as to how to work.

These were my words, January, 1888, and although Mr. Frith did not acknowledge the fact, there can be little doubt that the following passage in his " Further Reminiscences," page 335, referred to my remarks :—" I fear it is impossible in England to adopt the French system of the large atelier presided over by one or two distinguished artists. Instead of that method of teaching by which the student is directed by one man, and always on the same principles, we have in our Royal Academy teachers (Academicians and Associates) succeeding each other every month ; the effect being, in my opinion, confusion and bewilderment to the student. When this has been discussed amongst us, it has been urged that the clever student will listen to such varying advice and derive benefit from the differences in it ; while the stupid student who is bewildered will never make an artist at all. But we have to consider results, and there can be no doubt that the French student draws better, and is more generally accomplished in his art, than the English one ; and it behoves us to find out the reason and mend our method."

HIS MAJESTY GEORGE III. being pleased to establish A SOCIETY for the purpose of benefiting a few privileged OIL PAINTERS, SCULPTORS, and ARCHITECTS in 1768, under the NAME and TITLE of

THE ROYAL ACADEMY OF "CERTAIN" ARTS,

and HIS MAJESTY having hurriedly entrusted the sole management and direction of the Art of England to a CLIQUE composed of forty Academicians, with power to do whatever they please,

Hit therefore,

The President and Members of the said Clique, by virtue of our antiquated power, and in consideration of your being a very indifferent Engraver, copying our pictures, do, by our unique power, ignore all the talents in WATER-COLOUR PAINTING and BLACK-AND-WHITE, and, without a blush, constitute and appoint you,

.... Gentleman,

To be one of the ASSOCIATES of the Royal Academy, Hereby granting you all the privileges thereof, with which you can play any larks you like, so long as, with us, you ignore all advancement in other and more modern Arts.

LADY OIL, President.   R. A.   R. TAPE, Secretary.
                              APRIL 1st,
                              189......

THIS seems to me a fitting place to insert a parody of the diploma given to the artist when he is elected an Associate of the Royal Academy. The inscription on the blue ribbon of the R.A. is really "*Labor et Ingenium.*" Why not substitute "*Otium cum Dignitate*"? Once elected, the favoured one is surely at "rest," and would never dream of sullying the "honour."

> • " All those who're Out find fault with those who're In—
>   Till they're elect ; then deem all censure sin.
>   Who, Out, their venom on the R.A. spent,
>   Once In, with all its ways are quite content."

The medallion in the centre of the design is a faithful copy of the original. I give you my translation of it above, and if the Royal Academy likes the design they are quite at liberty to adopt it. What think you of it? Britannia at last points to Art recognising Water-Colour and Black-and-White, to the disgust of the three ugly sisters, Lady Oil, Sculpture, and Architecture. Poor little Engraving has collapsed in the presence of her "great automatic rival, the Sun," and is no longer seen. The British Lion is waking up from his one hundred and twenty years of sleep : "the patient animal seems fairly roused at last."

* Soden, "Rap at the R.A."

NO OTHERS NEED APPLY.

Election Antics.

THE antics of the Royal Academy in electing members to their body are more like the feminine proceedings of a girls' school than the business dealings of gentlemen. Until recently the cliquism that misguided their doings was quite unworthy of the representative professional artists of England. Perhaps this results from the fact that artists, unlike other professional men, have, with few exceptions, "fallen up " like Topsy.

The typical artist has but one subject of conversation—" Shop, shop, shop!" and dull shop, too. Next to singers and actors, painters are the most uninteresting and least informed of professional men; an evening in an art club will suffice to prove this to anyone. I mean nothing offensive in saying this; artists are a hard-working set of men, as a rule, and absorption in their work early in life leaves them no time or gives them no opportunity of mixing with men of the world. A glance at the curious specimens of humanity that collect together at an artists' soirée is sufficient to show the student of human nature the dear, clever, hard-working artist is not of the every-day world, and ought to be protected and provided for, not by members of their own calling, but by sympathetic men of the outer world free from eccentricities and prejudices.

I may inform the reader that this volume is written for the public ; the artists know my facts only too well, and need not be reminded that the governing body of the Royal Academy has been until recently cut up into cliques, and that the elections were seldom on the broad lines of ordinary merit, but were generally worked for the benefit of one small clique or the other.

A few years ago, at the time most of the present men were elected, this paltry game was played fast and furious. We had the St. John's Wood clique, the Kensington clique, the Hampstead clique, the Chelsea clique, and so on. The Scotch clique carried all before them for years ; indeed, I firmly believe, had I —when a younger man—daubed in violent colours, and adopted my mother's maiden name, MacKenzie, I should now have been " one of them."

To prove how absurd sometimes the " system " is still (absurd is rather too mild a term for this antic), I recall the election of one, whose name I will not give as he is still a member of the body and a very good fellow ; probably it was because of his being a good fellow he was elected. He belonged to—let us say—the Turn 'em Green clique, and as they were in power that particular year, they elected their good fellow. The election took place just after the annual exhibition had been hung, and when the name of the elected came to light, it was discovered the Turn-'em-out clique were the " hangers " that year, and had sent the work of the " good fellow " to the dark cellars below, marked with a " x " signifying " rejected "!

Does this tend to prove they can manage their own affairs ? Either the selecting council were wrong in rejecting the artist's work, or the electing body wrong in selecting him. This complication is the best reply to my query.

The year before last (1888) they rejected—not " doubtful," mark you—but rejected at once, so it is said, as not worthy of

consideration, Mr. Wyllie's picture of "The Flying Dutchman."
He sent the same picture last year; and, after he was elected a
member of the Academy, it was on the line.

Associates' Antics.

THE first symptoms of that disease known as Royal Academy fever manifest themselves in the typical artist when he

has been elected an Associate,
and he thinks he is now in the
running to be chosen one of the
inner circle.

His old Bohemian days are
quickly forgotten; the clay pipe
is discarded for the cigarette;
the old velveteen coat for Poole's
latest cut. This is a latter-day
fashion. The coat now makes
the artist; he is Fashion's spoilt
child. Snubs are now changed
to smiles, and the painter who
used to be ignored is now
idolised. The fact is, the old prejudice against artists is happily

THE OLD STYLE.

fast dying out; simply because practical paterfamilias, finding
the studio quite as profitable as the counting-house, welcomes
the artist craft, as furnishing a career for his son, as readily as
he does the Church, the Army, or the Bar.

That this prejudice still lingers to some extent, however, is
evident from the fact that the political Diogenes, in his search
for a model member of Parliament, has never but once thought
of the artist; and whilst brewers and poets, and such-like, are
welcomed to the Upper House, artists are left out in the cold.

For this prejudice the lady novelist is to some extent accountable. Her marionettes are handed down as sacred heirlooms from novel to novel.

The stereotyped wicked marquis, the injured governess, and the flighty ballet-girl, she may dangle before us without hurting anyone ; but the artist puppet—long-haired, ill-dressed, in seedy velvet coat and slouch hat, with empty brains and pocket, and the inevitable pot of beer and clay pipe—although he may exist, is out of the running. The world of art now only prospers in the world of fashion, and the Bohemian, like the poor relation, is voted a nuisance.

THE NEW STYLE.

The Associate attacked with Royal Academy fever has to diet himself—that is, he must by hook or by crook meet members of the Royal Academy at dinner. Then his pleasant house near Primrose Hill is considered on the wrong soil for the fever, and he must move to Kensington or Mayfair. He must avoid 'buses, taking carriage exercise instead ; he must build a studio an inch larger than his rival's, figure at Mrs. Lyon Hunter's " At Homes," give " At Homes " himself, and fly from home, anywhere, anywhere out of plebeian London, when fashion goes.

He is elected !

The worst of this malady is that when it leaves the patient, like other diseases it leaves *sequelæ* behind it. I fear, in most cases degeneration sets in ["Pot-Boiling" is the technical term], and that R.A. which might have stood for "Right ahead," now signifies "Rattle away."

His first relapse is the picture he has to give the Academy when he is elected. Nothing could show better this degeneration than a visit to the Royal Academy Chamber of Horrors, officially called "the Diploma Gallery."

There is, in my opinion, something very sad in the great lack of ideas in the pictures of our painters. First paint your picture, then find the subject, is, I assure you, generally their *modus operandi.* The painter when in doubt makes a study from

a pretty model, languishing eyes, big hat, and small waist. "Sure to sell;" and now that the artist is a full-blown R.A., his wares are all in the front window. Picture-painting "becomes merely the manufacture, in slightly varying forms, of some trick of effect or manipulation which the artist has made his own, and which, having been recognised as a success, is repeated *ad infinitum* at little expenditure of thought or feeling." The R.A. ("Rattle away") epidemic is too evident in many cases. How often do we see clever conscientious painters go to pieces once they are elected! How many cases can be noted of the reverse effect? Hardly any. Surely this proves that the academic system is a wrong one. It is wrong every way it is looked at. No private set of men should have it in their power to gratuitously damn the reputation of a professional man, simply because he

SAFE TO SELL.

may not be privately all that is pleasant to them, although his work may be vastly superior to that of his judges. On the other hand, how wrong it is to elect a mediocrity, and endow him for

the rest of his life with exceptional privileges ! There should be
no life members ; all ought to come up for re-election, like
members of Parliament, town councillors, or any governing
body properly constituted. But this is digression. I was men-
tioning artists' lack of ideas ; I should like to say a word about
their lack of originality of style as well as subject.

Look at the present realistic school —better call it the school
of ugliness—which ignores Keats' line, " A thing of beauty is a
joy for ever," and paints pictures of nasty, dirty people, in the
most approved French style. It is a matter of taste. Speaking
for myself, I prefer to gaze upon a beautiful girl, rather than on
a commonplace, uncleanly, uninteresting family being married,
or buried, or shipwrecked, or whitewashed—I mean painted.

The pretty, conventional school is old ; this ugly, realistic
school is new. Our forefathers had art served up to them like a
French dish—very pleasing,
but tasting of nothing one
knows, and not very satisfying.
In the days when that beautiful young man, so familiar to
all of us, walked out of a cos-
tumier's shop to make his last
appeal at the village well to
that charming young lady
fresh from the dancing academy, their ugly brothers and
sisters, in thick muddy boots
and unbecoming costumes,
were ignored by artists. I
think it is an artist's mission
to seek the beautiful, and

FROM THE PRETTY SCHOOL.

paint it ; but he must go to nature for it, not to fashion books.

That great artist, that immortal genius, Fred Walker, showed
how it was to be done. It is just as bad to be too pretty and
conventional, as it is to ignore, brutally ignore, all that is pleasing, and deride all the graceful conventionalities of art.

If painters work honestly they have their own style, for there is no doubt that no two painters see through the same glasses. I shall never forget how forcibly this fact struck me in Venice. I arrived at the city in the sea one Easter Sunday morning at sunrise, and, as my gondola glided down the Grand Canal, I was dazed with the beauty of the scene, and Turner was revealed to me in all his grandeur ; and, although I saw St. Mark's as Miss Montalba paints it, in miserable rain, and visited the lagoons in a perfect Whistler sea-mist, I prefer to dream of Venice as seen under the limelight of Turner's magnificence.

The Venetian Antic.

BUT there has sprung up lately a band of merry artists, all exceedingly clever, who see Venice through one painter's glasses —Van Haanen's. This remarkable painter, a superb artist of his kind, seems to act the part of Harlequin in that wonderful transformation of English artists into Venetian, now so popular at the Theatre Royal Academy. His influence is magical, for in whatever line our promising young artists select to display their talent, and whatever individuality they may have, it vanishes under his wand. They go to Venice.

Plain English Tom, Dick, and Harry, they return Van Tommaso, Van Ricardo, and Van Henrico—in fact, virtually, Van Haanen.

I am reminded of the anecdote of a Royal Academician who went abroad for a month or two. When he returned home, to the astonishment of his family he had contracted a strong foreign accent. No doubt, had he taken an excursion ticket to Venice, he would have added to his foreign accent this foreign style of painting.

One of our most talented young Royal Academicians made his name by his forcible realistic pictures of English life, rugged and true. But, alas! the Venetian candle was too attractive, his wings of originality were singed ; although his adopted ones may please for form and colour, he is lost, for a time, as a forcible painter of our own people and our own period. I have remarked before, it is the artist's mission to seek the beautiful, and when he has found it to paint it ; but why idealise unsavoury foreigners, as these artists who paint in Venice do, in place of staying at home and idealising our own people ?

The kennel and the nursery have supplied our painters with endless material for the manufacture of paying pictures. The Rattle-away Academician may be attracted to that school, so popular of late years, and paint puppies and babies—such subjects having left their proper place in the pages of toy-books (the delight of children, and jumped into frames (the delight of mammas). These painters may say Landseer transgressed in like manner. Landseer no doubt over-humanised his pets in pictures. But this great painter had a mission. He endowed animals with human sympathy to gain our sympathy for them.

Now what sympathy can we have for mischievous puppies which cannot exist, mere pantomime properties, and such as are represented by clever circus contortionists ? Of course, I exempt from these painters, artists like Millais, Riviere, and Burton Barber.

But sooner or later the Royal Academician or Associate, through *ennui*, finds refuge in portrait-painting. However, that is a subject I intend to treat in a companion volume of antics to this, so I shall not pursue the matter here.

I suppose we must feel sorry for the unfortunate artists. The Academy elect Associates, and then leave them practically branded failures. The terrible slight may be in some cases the artist's own fault—too much " Rattle away ; " but generally it is the Academic failure of judgment, and the result of the whole system. If A. for Associate really means Approval, and the A. has not staying power, then after a certain time he should retire. But, bless me, why should I trouble myself offering suggestions to the present Royal Academy? This will all be right when the R.A. is a thing of the past, and we have a National

Academy, managed by the State, for the people and for Art in general.

Mr. Clint was the only artist in the past who ever voluntarily withdrew from the ranks of the Royal Academy. He pursued a manly course. "He was elected an Associate in 1821, and after fourteen years of waiting for election into the highest ranks of the Academy, he in 1835 resigned his diploma. He would no longer, he said, suffer himself to remain in a position which enabled his brethren to depreciate his talents. He had seen twenty vacancies occur, and had seen them filled up in some few instances by his seniors, but in most cases by his juniors in point of election and, we will add, talent. Between 1821 and 1835 the Academy had been able to elect into its ranks two-and-twenty Associates, viz., Clint, Wyattville, Jones, Pickersgill, Wilkins, Etty, Danby, Allen, Briggs, E. Landseer, Deering, Chalon, Eastlake, Newton, Cockerill, Witherington, Wyon, Stanfield, Geddes, Gibson, Unwins, and Lee. Of these twenty-two all have been or are, with three exceptions, Royal Academicians. The exceptions are Mr. Geddes, who died an Associate; Mr. Danby, who is still (1854) an Associate; and Mr. Clint, who withdrew in 1835. It was Mr. Clint's belief that the prospects of an artist are seriously injured by any body of men who can at every fresh vacancy pass a slur upon his talents by electing his junior to that position which it is evident to the public he is anxious to obtain. Nay, Mr. Clint would urge, and did urge vehemently at the time, that an artist should not be elected an Associate unless it was clear to those who elected him that he had even then painted pictures of merit enough to entitle him to the full honours of the Academy. Our wonder is not that Mr. Clint withdrew, but that he was so long in withdrawing." Now it is no matter in what way his prospects were injured; it is enough that he has painted pictures; that they will live from their own high merits, and the able actors they perpetuate, while oil and canvas will hold together, and after the Royal Academy has fallen to pieces.

Selecting and Hanging Antics.

THE Selecting and Hanging Antics have been so well ventilated that I fear it would bore my reader to repeat them. I sincerely sympathise with the unfortunate Royal Academicians whose lot it is to "do their duty to their house and country" in these committees. The fact is, they have too much to do. Nearly 12,000 works of art pass before them for their careful judgment in about twelve days; this is at the rate of much over a hundred an hour. Why, the incessant stream of gilt frames and painting would daze a lizard, and after a time colour-blindness must ensue, and injustice, unintentional, must occur. Why not limit the number of pictures allowed in for competition to two from each person, as in the Salon, thus making the artists choose their best work only, and prevent their sending in eight, as they often do now, on the chance of having one—and probably that the worst one—placed? The Royal Academicians increase this evil-working trouble four-fold by inviting so much work. Though doubtless, as things are, they do their best, they are entirely at a loss how to master this difficulty;* and being a clique, in place of an open representative body, they are liable to give dissatisfaction, and my only solution to the matter is for the Burlington House Happy Family to keep to themselves, and show all their wares, and give up the "Royal" instrument (a magnet which draws all fashion and money to them) to the body of English

* "You find that you want space very much?"—"Very much indeed."

I imagine it would not be saying too much to say that, in fact, you are compelled reluctantly sometimes to do injustice to individual artists, not from any want of inclination to do them justice, but solely because the space at your disposal is so extremely small?"—"I should like to have room enough to hang all the pictures that come to us from the Council. *Not a year passes but some pictures are turned away that ought to have good places, because they are too good to go in bad places.*"

"Space is urgently required?"—"Yes, and I think also the number of pictures allowed to be sent by Academicians and Associates should be limited."

"Would you think four enough?"—"I think four would be plenty."

"I think the hanging is done far too hurriedly."—EVIDENCE OF W. P. FRITH, R.A., BEFORE ROYAL COMMISSION, 1863.

E

This is a purely imaginary picture, drawn according to the accounts given of the scene by members of the Royal Academy Selecting Committee. The Author applied this year for admission, but his request was refused, although the privilege of being present for the purpose of sketching has been granted to a foreign artist.

SELECTING. (*According to Mr. Cope, R.A.*)

artists, to open a National Academy, large
enough, and sufficiently competent to deal
with the necessities of the tremendous growth
of our art in England.

How does this hurry-skurry selection scene
compare with the historical picture by Mr. Cope
(exhibited 1876)?—no difficult subject to cope
with ; but let me open my mind with the aid
of this key, and point out what I see in this
vigorous scene of "hurry-skurry selection."

The ever-delightful, bluff Sir John Millais
sits in the foreground, impatient, no doubt,
to get off to the Garrick Club card-room.
Opposite to him sits the present keeper
of the R.A., Mr. Calderon, hat in hand,
ready to fling it at the atrocious work
languidly presented for inspection. Behind
him stands the breezy Mr. Hook, whose
weather-eye is upon the Spaniard, and
ready to arrest the hand when raised to
throw the wideawake.

To the left of the picture observe the elder Mr. Richmond about to sit down upon Sir Frederick (then Mr.) Leighton's hat. Sir Francis Grant, President, you may notice, is not looking at the picture, but watches the action of the head carpenter in the Scotch cap, who is evidently contemplating having a shy at the President's hat with a lump of chalk which he holds in his hands, merely to relieve the monotony of his occupation, which consists generally in making a great big x (rejected) on the back of the unfortunate outsider's work. The President is saying to himself, "Try it, Mr. Carpenter, and you'll get this hammer at your head." All the rest look horribly bored; but I understand the picture has found a resting-place in the Diploma Gallery, a surrounding in keeping with the prevailing sadness.

It is only of late years that the Royal Academy has had the politeness to send by post the notification to the artists about the fate of their pictures. This considerate body used to ignore outsiders' interests and feelings altogether, and on a certain day all outsiders had to crowd to the Academy, and scramble to find out from the "Book of Fate" in the Hall whether their work was in or out. It is little better now. Artists certainly get a card —one year it was a post-card!—but it is not until they arrive at Burlington House on Varnishing Day that they know the precise fate of their pictures.

Varnishing=Day Antics.

IT is a brave Royal Academician that faces the crowd of artists streaming into Burlington House on "Varnishing Day" from north, south, east, and west, by road, river, and rail—that is, if he happens to be one of the Council of the year, and responsible for the selection and hanging.

He flinches from meeting the man he has "hung" high, who may upbraid him for such unfairness, and turns away to avoid the effusive thanks of the friend he has placed "on the line," with all the injustice with which it may be fraught to the clever stranger.

The annual tales of this unfairness, if collected, would make a volume ten times as large as this, and such an indictment of the Royal Academy that all fair-minded Englishmen would cease to have any respect for that body, and quickly see the necessity of taking away from this clique the power of damning an artist's reputation.

Were Englishmen less phlegmatic, we might have "scenes" in the Royal Academy on Varnishing Day. Although the French Salon is managed on much fairer lines (*see* page 58), the national temperament will show itself. A few years ago a disappointed artist was so enraged when he discovered his master-piece "skied" in the Salon, he smothered it completely with black paint.

So very French, you know!

Can it be true that an American bought it, on the first day, as a Nocturne, by an impressionist?

Ask Mr. Whistler.

Mons. Vifficile, finding his favourite work slighted in the same way, rushed madly up the ladder, drew his knife, and cut his picture clean out of the frame, and walked away with it.

How I wish some of his English brethren would follow his example—say, some of our antiquated R.A.'s ; but, alas ! they do not cut up their pictures—the critics do that for them.

Academicians and Associates have three days to "varnish" their pictures or re-paint them ; outsiders only have one, and what antics the R.A.'s and the A.R.A.'s can play in three days ! Why, they not only have had the privilege of hanging their work pretty much as they like, but should any outsider's work tell against theirs, they can knock Mr. or Mrs. Outsider silly, by painting in a bright sky, a killing green, or a vile red coat at the last moment ; and to complete the joke, some of them cover *their* picture over with a cloth, so that when Mr. and Mrs. Outsider, who are allowed one day, arrive (and I have seen the poor outsiders struggling to make the most of the few paltry hours allotted to them in a fog !) *they* cannot see what the R.A.'s or A.R.A.'s picture is like, and therefore cannot touch up their work so that it may hold its own. Cry "Shame ! shame !" at this unfairness !

Certainly, matters used to be even worse ! Yes ; even more contemptible and more unfair. Outsiders were not

O. SLAPHASH RA

A VERY "ARTISTIC JOKE.

allowed to touch up their pictures at all ! You doubt it ? Here is the evidence of Mr. George Rennie before the Royal Commission, 1836.

"The admission or exclusion is decided by the Council."

"Suppose they exclude or admit, as they think proper, the next process is the ' private view ' ? "

"That is the private view after the Exhibition is arranged. The Academicians reserve all the best places, and, also by Regulation No. 8, three days or more, according to the discretion of the Council, shall be allowed to the members of the R.A. to finish and paint their pictures in the places that have been alloted to them I believe there is no rule more complained of, nor which is a greater grievance."

"Other artists, not Academicians, have not the power of retouching their pictures?"

"No, the Academician has the sole privilege of admission to the Exhibition rooms, where he may re-touch and finish his pictures and clean them; in fact, he may put them in the very best condition to be seen, whereas an artist who is not an Academician submits his pictures to the public view, dusty, dirty, and in whatever situation they may remain after the dust and bustle of preparing the Exhibition is over. In the Sculpture Room I have seen busts and statues in marble with the ten dirty finger-marks of the porter covering their faces, which the exhibitor has not had the opportunity of washing."

AFTER THE FAIR.

The statue as it appeared when ex-   The same statue—I exhibited
hibited by a Royal Academician or   by an outsider.
Associate.

I have endeavoured in this sketch to show you the effect, but I would require colour to show the result produced by R.A.'s and A.R.A.'s in three days' painting on their work after it is hung, to the detriment of the outsiders. Of course you will be told by Academicians that they cover up their pictures to save them from dust; but surely they ought to be prompted by common fairness to allow the painters of the *neighbouring pictures* to see the general effect, and not throw dust in *their* eyes.

A SUGGESTION FOR A MECHANICAL PRESIDENT TO CART AWAY THE RUBBISH OF ROYAL ACADEMICIANS IN ORDER TO MAKE ROOM FOR GOOD WORK BY OUTSIDERS.

I feel sure the following childish antic is authentic, for it is related by one who writes with authority as well as with singular ability on art matters :—

"By the way, I hear that when the serious work of hanging was at an end, on the last of the three days devoted to members' varnishing, Gallery No. III at the Royal Academy presented a very comic appearance. No doubt my readers are all familiar by this time with the quaint manners and customs of a mechanical toy which has made quite a sensation in the London streets during the last four or five weeks. I mean a small tin man, who solemnly draws along a little cart, gradually 'slowing up,' according to the requirements of his internal machinery, with a sedate gravity which is exceedingly amusing. It seems, however, that the members of the Royal Academy were not even aware of the existence of this toy; and when a certain Associate brought one out of his pocket towards the end of the day's work on Thursday in last week, and, gravely winding it up, set it walking down the centre of the big room, brushes and palettes were laid aside, varnishing was heeded not, and the artists with one accord watched the little toy with the most babyish delight. It must have been comic to see these 'potent, grave, and reverend signors' following with their eyes the mechanical man and his cart. Here would have been a rare chance for the sarcastic pencil of Mr. Harry Furniss to represent the Royal Academy under an entirely novel aspect."

I have too much respect for the writer to refuse.

Landscape artists have from time to time seriously complained of injustice at the hands of the Royal Academy. Can we wonder at this when we come across the following list of the Royal Academy Council of Selection for one year?

Portrait Painters 4
Figure Painters............. 3
Animal Painter............... 1
Engraver 1

While landscape, the representative and strongest of English painting, whether in oil or water-colour, is not represented at all! No doubt there are many similar cases to this, and a few years ago one ill-treated landscape painter, smarting under injustice, had the impudence to write a letter to the *Times.* The policy of Royal Academicians is not to notice outside criticism. And it is a wise policy on their part; for whenever they take up the cudgels to defend themselves, they generally come off second best. Such was proved to be the truth in this case. Mr. E. Armitage, R.A., a member of the Hanging Committee of the year, rushed out in a rage to meet the audacious member of the " Outside Legion of Landscape Artists " who dared to say (and say rightly, at the time) that the Academicians as a body had an imperfect sympathy with landscape; but the R.A. had to retire with the public verdict against him. One passage in the R.A.'s defence ought to be "writ large" on Burlington House. " I think it right to point out to your correspondent, and the school to which he belongs, how useless are their protests against the Council of the Royal Academy"! and adds, " It is not my

wish to defend the Hangers of the year." Was there ever a
better illustration of Might being Right?

I'll take you into the centre of any gallery, and ask you how
many pictures are hung in the room. Probably you begin to
count from a "skied" one on your left all round to the "skied"
one on your right. Nonsense! not more than six works are
really hung in the gallery where we stand, or in any gallery
except the large ones, where a few more are accommodated.

The system of hanging is simply this. The "centres" of the
rooms are first arranged, and with "principal" pictures, or pictures
by privileged painters; the remainder are arranged merely to show
these "centres" off to the best advantage. Probably you will
say, " So as the pictures are on the line, what does it matter?"
Pray reflect. The "centres" have to be "hung up to," or
" played up to " (for want of a better term). A glowing sunset
will have cold-toned pictures all round it to make it brilliant, and
so on. So you are struck with the favoured few pictures—either
that such wretched work should be honoured so, or by the real
artistic effect upon you. But you little think how that effect is
produced, or what injustice is done to others so as to arrive at it.
Now in the Salon they re-hang the Exhibition when half the
time is over, and therefore all pictures have a chance. " Why
do not the Academicians do so also? " Ah! now I see you are
beginning to question, and to find out their selfishness. Now
look around—see: portraits! portraits! portraits everywhere!

" Why? "

"Because portrait painters are the greatest salesmen. Many
rich people only get painted by a member of the Royal Academy
on the understanding their portrait shall be exhibited. And the
worst of it is, the sort of people who, by means of a ' thumping
cheque ' to a Royal Academician, and for purposes of unmerited
notoriety, get their portraits hung at our annual Art shows, are
almost invariably quite commonplace, and are generally very
ugly."

" What do you suggest to remedy this? "

" The only remedy for all the evil of the Royal Academy is

to have a National Academy of Art, directed by the State, and let the present Royal Academy, if it is a public body, amalgamate; if it is not, let it take its chance with the other private shows."

" But you could not exclude portraits ? "

"Certainly not. But I would have a separate gallery for them—an annual National Portrait Gallery. The Council to select the works of artistic merit only, and not any rubbish because a Royal Academician painted it, as is the case now."

" You seem to place the Academy on a par with any other gallery."

" Oh dear no! That would not be fair to the other galleries. I repeat, the Royal Academy is merely a gigantic sale-room, in which each member has the privilege of having the best space to show his own wares. They take all the money they can, as a public body, get rent free ; as a private body, show no balance-sheet ; and, apart from their handful of scholars and pensioners, do nothing whatever for the advancement of Art."

I must admit there has been an effort on the part of Academicians (no doubt in consequence of adverse criticism) to treat the outsiders better. Last year Messrs. Stone and Fildes worked with that object ; but the fact is, the outsiders are getting stronger every year, and the Royal Academy is getting weaker.

" I understood the Academy was exactly the same as it always has been ? "

" That is the point. Exactly the same after one hundred and twenty years ! Fancy that ! Nothing has increased more than Art in that time, and yet while all old, rusty institutions have been altered, and moved with the times, the Royal Academy alone remains the small, conceited, unsatisfactory body it has always been."

𝔄𝔫𝔱𝔦𝔠𝔰 𝔴𝔦𝔱𝔥 𝔖𝔠𝔲𝔩𝔭𝔱𝔲𝔯𝔢.

THE great joke my Lady Oil has with her sister of clay or marble is that her works are not properly seen. Paintings might just as well be hung on the outer walls of Burlington House as large subjects in sculpture crowded together in a small gallery. Until the Royal Academy cover over the court-yard with glass, and place the sculpture there, we cannot judge properly of the undoubted merits of our sculptors. See how charming the

CHANTREY.

works look at the Salon, arranged in a huge glass building, shown to every advantage !

Surely our sculptors have enough to contend against, with our climate unsuited for their material, and our people devoid of a proper appreciation of their work. An average Englishman's soul for sculpture does not rise higher than those petrified tailor's dummies, presentation statues of a mayor or an M.P., or very occasionally a man of genius, which we find sprinkled over the country.

I feel sure that had we a proper National Academy for current art, and could we see the really fine works many of our sculptors produce, native appreciation for sculpture would be developed, and an end would come to the abortions in marble that make our public statues the laughing stock of the art world.

A Sculptor's Antic is one of the few antics that we can put to the credit of the Royal Academicians. This was played many years ago by one Sir Francis Chantrey, to the pleasant tune of leaving in his will provision for a yearly sum of money for the "Encouragement of BRITISH FINE ART in PAINTING and SCULPTURE." The bequest came into force in 1877. Of course in Chantrey's day the best pictures were for sale off the walls of the Royal Academy, but now the President and Council have to choose practically from those pictures and works in exhibitions which the dealers have not bought, for they must not give commissions. The consequence is that there have already been one or two signs of the Royal Academy coming to the rescue of a member of their body thrown out of the sales of the year. A trick of this kind that happened a few years ago would have made the shade of the testator turn in his grave. I am informed that the Royal Academy at first thought the bequest was intended for the encouragement chiefly of outsiders, so they hesitated to buy any of their own works; but later on legal opinion pronounced in favour of Academic work being available as well. Truly it would have been more noble on their part to act according to the *spirit* and not according to the *letter* of the will.

Architectural Antics.

LADY OIL has always treated her sister Architecture well.
She provided for her in her original " instrument," and favoured
her ever since.   Still, there is no doubt that architectural outsiders
are just as dissatisfied with the present state of affairs as artists
are, and yearn for a truly representative National Academy.
A Fellow of the Royal Institute of British Architects unburdens
his soul as follows, in a letter to the *Pall Mall Gazette* of
May 5th, 1887 : —

   " Few people during the past fifteen years," says the writer, " have had more
works accepted at Burlington House than I have, so that the complaint I am going to
make cannot be ascribed to what Sir F. Leighton calls ' embitterment.'   One little
room in the whole series of sixteen galleries at the Royal Academy of Arts is devoted
to the representation of architecture, necessarily the leading, and certainly the oldest,
of the fine arts.   Here, therefore, one might with good reason surely expect to see
illustrations of buildings of the year ; but this clearly is far from the case on the
present occasion, inasmuch as by far the larger part of the available space on the line
is occupied by young students' designs or their holiday sketches of " old bits."   The
Queen's Great Hall of the Palace for East London is poked down so low as to render
it necessary for the visitor to go on hands and knees to see it at all correctly.   *One
young gentleman who happens to be a pupil of an eminent R.A. has seven of his Con-
tinental sketches of mediæval work well hung,* and yet the Birmingham Law Courts,
of which the Queen laid the foundation stone a short time since, are not represented
at all.   Only one of the three designs for the Liverpool Cathedral is exhibited—

namely, Messrs. Bodley and Garner's; and the drawing of that, which is a very fine one, is put under the cornice, almost, if not quite, out of sight, several speculative designs being placed on the line below on the same wall. Could anything be more unfair and really foolish, especially when dozens of good drawings of erected buildings are sent away from the same gallery?"

The writer of this is an architect, and quite right to assert that, in his opinion, architecture is the leading fine art ; but that is no reason the Royal Academy should favour architecture at the expense of England's finest art—water-colour. I detest the present absurd childish cry of class against mass, and would be sorry to see it introduced in art controversies, but I will ask the radical Mr. Marcus Stone to compare the following published statements, which I print side by side to show that something very like favouritism has existed, if it does not exist now, in the society aristocratic body of which he is a member:—

THE TWIST HAND.

"Henry Dawson began life as a 'twist hand' in a lace factory at Northampton, but the love of art manifesting itself, he devoted his spare time to the study of painting, and adopted art as his profession in 1835. In 1844 he went to Liverpool, and in 1849 removed to Croydon, where he painted some of his finest works. From Croydon Mr. Dawson went to Thorpe, where he painted the noble picture of the Houses of Parliament. Throughout his career, till a very few years back, the artist struggled on the borders of poverty, through the lowness

THE LANDED PROPRIETOR.

"The name of Mr. John Peter Deering, R.A., is little known as connected with art, except to those who may have seen it among the list of members of the Royal Academy, as printed in their annual catalogue (died 1850) ; and they who have done so have probably marvelled however it came there. Mr. J. P. Deering, who was known as Mr. J. P. Gandy in earlier life, was an architect, and, we believe, a younger brother of Mr. Joseph Gandy, also an architect, and an Associate of the Academy. According to the *Athenæum*, Mr. Deering began life under of the prices at which he was obliged to sell his pictures. At the Academy his works were either rejected, skied, or floored. The closing of the old British Institution, where Mr. Dawson's pictures were always well placed, was a serious blow to him; so also was the failure of a movement (through the death of his friend John Philp) to redress the injustice of his exclusion from the Academic ranks. At length, in 1872-73, when the artist was past sixty, his works were for the first time placed on the line at the Academy; and, almost concurrently, the market price of his works increased in a proportion which has had few parallels. As a single example of this rise in prices we may mention that the 'Wooden Walls,' which in 1852 was bought from the artist for £75, sold in Christie's in 1876 for £1,400. Mr. Dawson will, I believe, rank in the history of our school but little, if at all, after Crome, Müller, Cox, and other of our long inadequately appreciated masters."

the patronage of the Dilettanti Society, and by that society undertook a professional mission to Greece. With the exception of Exeter Hall in the Strand, we are not aware of any important edifice designed and erected by him. Yet in 1827 he was elected an Associate of the Academy, having in that year succeeded to considerable landed property in Buckinghamshire. In 1838 he was chosen Academician, though for the five preceding years he had not exhibited a drawing at their Exhibitions; nor has there been one since, a period of seventeen years (1850). Mr. Deering sat in the first reformed Parliament for the borough of Aylesbury. He was fond of his art, and if he had been a poorer man he would have become distinguished in it. The election of Mr. Deering into full membership is one of the 'mistakes' which the Royal Academy has sometimes made; the retention of its honours by this gentleman seventeen years after he had *de facto* quitted his profession, was neither creditable to him nor should it have been permitted by the society."

The corner room given to Sister Architecture is only patro-
nised by old ladies, who take refuge in it to devour the contents
of their luncheon baskets ; fat old gentlemen who wish to get
cool; and thin young men who want to get married, and can
spoon undisturbed.

The last-named have a splendid chance of leading up to the
burning question, by selecting a " design for a church " on the
walls—unless he happens to be a painter in Water-Colour or
Artist in Black-and-White, who takes his *fiancée* into the room
to point out the injustice of electing "drawers of builders' plans,"
in place of Artists of genius.

F

THE CINDERELLAS OF THE ROYAL ACADEMY.

The Worst Antic of All.

I BRACKET the "Cinderellas" of the Royal Academy together —Water-Colour and Black-and-White; with the latter, of course, I include Etchers.

* The French Academy, the Salon, is not at all monopolised by painters in oil colours. My Lady Oil of Burlington House is a very selfish creature; she persistently refuses to recognise her twin-sister Water-Colour, giving her but one miserable room in her mansion, and no share whatever in her honours. My Lady Oil is selfish, my Lady Oil is unjust, to favour engravers and architects, and ignore painters in water-colour and artists in black-and-white. She showers honours on her adopted sisters Engraving and Architecture, because the former mechanically reproduces her work, and the latter builds her pretty toy-houses for her children to live in.

This is really altogether absurd when you reflect that it is in water-colour English art excels, and that the copyist, the engraver's occupation will soon be gone, beaten away by slightly more mechanical, but much more effective, modes of reproduction.†

Sooner or later John Bull will open his inartistic eyes, and see that mediocrity in oil is not equal to excellence in water, and that those who originate with the pencil are far before copyists with the graver, and drawers of plans.

Why, all the world knows that the great English water-colour masters have never had at any time any recognition whatever from oil-painters,‡ while the most competent and

* From my lecture "Art and Artists."

† "His great automatic rival, the Sun, will outshine him at last."—FRANCIS SEYMOUR HADEN, F.R.C.S., President of the Royal Society of Painter-Etchers.

‡ Evidence of Henry Warren, 1863, President of the New Society of Painters in Water-Colours :—

"Do you consider that the honours of the Academy are now as open to water-colour painters as to oil painters?"—"Certainly not. I never understood that they were open to water-colour painters at all. No water-colour painter that I know of has been elected a member."

Evidence of J. P. Knight, R.A. :—

"At the present moment, as we understand the rule of the Academy, water-colour

F 2

impartial judges pronounced water-colour to be England's most original art. Think of the names of De Wint, Cox, William Hunt, Barret, Fielding, Holland, Prout, Varley, Chambers, Girtin, Turner, John Lewis, Cattermole, among the rest! Turner and Lewis were R.A.'s because they painted in *oils* also.

Home Rule in Art has not improved matters. The Royal Hi-

A FAREWELL SYMPHONY BY HADEN.

bernian Academy and Scottish Academies follow in this respect the narrow-mindedness and selfishness of Lady Oil of Burlington House, showing clearly that a National Academy of the Union of Arts, presided over by a Minister of State, is the only remedy for this vulgar snub to England's greatest art.

Frank Sir John Millais, speaking of my friends and fellow-

painters are not admitted to the honours of the Academy."—"There is no rule excluding them. I think that if there were any water-colour painter of equal eminence to compete with the oil painters of his day he would be as likely to be elected as an oil painter." "Can you name a water-colour painter who as such has been elected? Do you think that distinction should be kept up or not?"—"Certainly not."

workers with the pencil, remarked that some of them are artistically superior to painters.

This I mildly expounded in a letter to the daily Press a year or two ago, and begged to state as my honest opinion that in any other country but ours John Tenniel, George du Maurier, and Charles Keene would be honorary members of a National Academy devoted to popular art.

An important critic, *à propos* of my letter, went further, and truly wrote, " One Tenniel is worth a wilderness of respectable R.A.'s, and there is more and better art in a single sketch signed ' C. K.' (Charles Keene) than in nine-tenths of the pictures in the Diploma Gallery put together."

Mr. Frith, who had evidently been reading current opinions, particularly mine, before writing his " Further Reminiscences," writes months after the above was spoken by me :—

" No man can have a keener sense of the merits of fine line or mezzotint engraving than the present writer, and no one less begrudges the honours of the Royal Academy to the distinguished men who at this time enjoy them : but when I see original designers of real genius pour forth with astonishing prodigality week after week, and month after month, works either in etching or on wood in which such difficulties in art as composition, character, expression, and light and shadow, are successfully surmounted, I feel a sense of shame that some honourable mark is not placed upon their producers. An engraver is but a translator after all ; and if the Academy admits, as, in my opinion, it does very properly, the translators, why not the originator in black-and-white, who displays in his works every quality of art except colour ? . . . If my ideas on the subject are correct, the compliment should be paid and a long-standing grievance redressed." *

Yet in the face of these published opinions of Sir John Millais and Mr. Frith—both active and important members of the Royal Academy—nothing whatever has been done to alter matters. So much for Royal Academicians' power to carry out their professed opinions.

The conviction that Black-and-White men should be elected is not confined to artists at random ; I take the utterances of a man of science. Sir Rutherford Alcock, K.C.B., presiding at an

* Mr. Frith's " Further Reminiscences," pp. 408-9.

SINCE WRITING THIS, MR. FRITH HAS RETIRED.

address on Etching at the Royal Institution (I think), spoke as follows :—" There was no doubt, if the Royal Academy of Art was, as every one understood, a society created especially to develop and foster Art, it should be catholic, large, and cosmopolitan."

Is it possible to have it catholic, large, and cosmopolitan unless the Royal Academy of Art is a national and not a private concern ?

THE WATER-COLOUR ROOM IS NEXT THE REFRESHMENT DEPARTMENT.
OBSERVE THE RESULT.

Entertaining Antics.

THE PRIVATE VIEW.

" Public views, called ' private,' where everybody goes,
To see and be seen by everybody that everybody knows."

WHY call it " Private " ? Surely there is nothing private about the
principal selling-day? Better call it " Free day;" but why free?
Why not charge the cream of wealth and fashion ten shillings
each, entrance money, and hand the takings over to the artists
charitable institutions? (A suggestion made by me in a letter
to the papers three years ago.) Are the Academicians afraid of
losing a chance customer by adopting my suggestion? They
charge extra for charitable purposes at the French Salon for
private views, and they open their Exhibition FREE to the
PUBLIC on Sunday afternoons ; but then the French understand
this, for they are a nation of artists. They say we are a nation
of shopkeepers. Well, there is nothing to be ashamed of in
that ; but there *is* in the fact that, with very few exceptions,
unkind critics might say our well-known artists are not artists,
but purveyors of painted canvases. This is not altogether the
artists' fault, but the nation's. By circumstance we are an inartistic nation ; by perversity we remain so. The nation buy up
the telegraphs ; the railways will follow. But will it ever buy up
the art, as the French and other nations do, and induce young
artists to foster ambition instead of affectation, and our older
ones grandeur instead of grabbing, and worship Art for Art's
sake?—not throwing themselves, as they do now, under the
wheels of the Juggernaut of Fashion.

The fact is, to our national disgrace, My Lady Oil revels
in being fashionable before everything else, and Fashion, which
leads public opinion by the nose, cares little for Art, and
perhaps knows nothing whatever about the exclusive private
body I call The Lady Oil. It is her ladyship's field day. She
has Fashion at her feet. The Royal Academy is Vanity Fair,

and that is all that Fashion cares about—as she goes there, not
to see, but to be seen. But if she has this little volume of mine
in her hands, I ask her to read the following extract carefully,
and when next she has

> " Noted well
> The dress and air of ev'ry belle
> Who came from country or from town
> To show her taste, or cap, or gown,"

think of my Lady Oil, and the poor outsider she has left in the
cold. Read what the *Times* says :—

"At least it should not be taken for granted that improvement is impossible till
improvement has been attempted. This much has been forced upon us by the painful

REJECTED " FOR WANT OF SPACE."

knowledge of the many bitter, often heartbreaking, disappointments which cloud the
opening of the Royal Academy Exhibition, when London looks bright and blooming,
and every one and everything around seems so full of life, and so eager and capable of
enjoyment. It is impossible for those whose office carries them behind the scenes, in
the midst of the festive and fashionable crowd which throngs the stately rooms of the
Academy, not to think of the poor lodging and the shabby studio, and the easel, the
rejected picture, the subject of so much labour, the spring of so many hopes, which
was expected to win bread, if not fame, for the painter."

As soon as the doors are open on " Private " view days we
hear the beating of the drum : "Walk up! walk up! ladies and

gentlemen! just a-goin' to begin! Buy! buy! buy! Come
early if you want the pick! Mor'n, Sir Crœsus. Something to
suit you? Plenty; don't look up, keep your eye on the line, we
are all on it. Buy! buy! buy! Here is Treackle Slapdash, R.A.
Six feet of paint, six thousand pounds; why, it's giving it away.
For your local gallery, eh? Oh, then you can have it for five
thousand five hundred; the advertisement I'll make of it is

worth an extra five hun-
dred! Walk up! Buy!
buy! buy! Ah, Mr.
Downey Dealer, you are
here early, but the early
Bond Street bird has
caught the worm; so
cut away at catalogue
prices, and come again.
Walk up! walk up!
Buy! buy! buy! How
do, my Lord Dobody?
You want something
too? Ah, just to talk
about it as your pur-
chase; I see. What's
to pay? Oh, we don't
bother about that; we

"WALK UP! WALK UP!"

don't force you to pay; don't protect the artist in any way. Of
course, we strike it off 'sold.' Walk up! walk up! walk up!
Ah, Lady Pedigreen, delighted to see you and your five
daughters, and your sisters, and your cousins, and your
aunts. Ah! Colonel Chiselhurst, come to see how your portrait
looks? There it is. Stand close to it, and have a field day all
to yourself. Walk up! walk up! Canon Flummery, walk up!
I think it is the fiery Furniss says paintings are texts for writers'
sermons. So you'll find plenty of texts—funny ones, some of
them—no sermon, please—but take notes for your speech at our
banquet. Something short and buttery, please. Ha, ha! my

R.A.'s and A.R.A.'s and families. Walk up! walk up! What a day we're having, to be sure!"

Mutual admiration antics follow, which are not worth the recording.

What am I to say about antics in buying and selling?

True, we have noble patrons still among us, but certainly not sufficient to buy a fraction of the works of 12,000 artists. The amateur gambling in pictures is lowering to true art, and the artist is naturally the one to suffer. It has become the habit —a most obnoxious, unworthy, and unprofessional one—to accept "offers" for pictures a great deal below the Catalogue price; so that artists are brought down to the level of Italian shopkeepers, and consequently imitate the unscrupulous foreigner by sticking on a first price to allow for the cutting down. The worst of this is the Academy will not protect the artist, or guarantee that the stranger (the Lord Dobody I mention on a former page) ever turns up or pays for the picture. The unfortunate artist loses the sale of his work; but this, mark you, is peculiar to the Royal Academy. Other Exhibitions guarantee the money to the artist, so that the occupant of "the poor lodging and the shabby studio," the struggling owner of the easel and "the *accepted* picture, the subject of so much labour," whose hopes are gladdened by hearing that his picture is sold by the Academy, and at last there is bread for his family, may have his hopes and profits dashed to the ground through any adventurer being allowed to falsely have the picture marked as "sold" to him, when it is merely, and possibly irresponsibly, bespoke!*

> * "When day is gone, and night is come,
> And all are laid to sleep,
> I think of little folks upstairs
> That I have got to keep—
> Oh dear!
> Who would not wake and weep?"—*Punch.*

A correspondent, a clever "rising artist," writes to me, suggesting "the desirableness of the R.A. charging a commission and taking the responsibility of the sale. My own case was that a certain Lord ———, who bought a picture on the *private view*, took no notice of any communication afterwards, and lost me the sale of the work for the season. This could not happen in any other Exhibition."

I maintain that no properly-constituted National Academy would tolerate this, and furthermore I hold that it would be the duty of a National Academy to purchase certain works from each Exhibition (as they do in France), and distribute these works in provincial museums and art galleries.

The Banquet Antics.

THE "MENOO."

THE Annual Banquet of the Royal Academy is a trade institution. Booksellers have their dinners, cheesemongers have theirs—why not the proprietors of an art store? It is to advertise their wares, and feast their patrons. Quite right—why not? But, my dear Lady Oil, be not misled ; reflect that when the "butter" is laid on too thick, ten to one it is nothing but margarine, which, like your high-flown antics, articulates about Art (with a very big **A**), but spells trade with a very small

t, and, moreover, can't be tasted. Are her ladyship's invitations representative or general? Read her list year after year, and judge for yourself, and pray read this statement by a writer in *Harper's Magazine,** and say if you believe it :—

"Not many years ago it was said that an ambitious amateur had spent £25,000 on the pictures of living artists, in the hope that his munificent patronage would procure him an invitation to the dinner at Burlington House; but his well-meaning efforts were unsuccessful, and he was not present at the banquet."

H'm. I should like to know if the £25,000 was spent in the purchase of works of Academicians or outsiders? If this foolish Crœsus spent all this money with the snobbish intent, it would be useless for his purpose in the pockets of outsiders; they cannot invite any one to the Art Trade Banquet. If he bribed the members, how mean of them knowingly to take the money and not give the poor snob his dinner; but if he spent his £25,000 on outsiders, then comment is superfluous. (As a matter of fact it was not "spent" at all, but only offered.)

The banquet, like the speeches, is heavy and dull—a striking contrast to the old days when David Garrick, George Colman, Samuel Foote, Burke, Johnson, Goldsmith, and others dined with the Royal Academy at the cost of five shillings a head. In those days no fool spent £25,000 to be asked, and no idiot was egotistical enough to slam the door in his face for offering to do so.

The principal banqueting antic of the Royal Academy is to snub their best friend the Press.† Only the representative of one daily paper is admitted, and if the other papers want a report of the banquet they must get it through that paper.

* I may mention the writer of this article in *Harper's* examined the minute-books and the archives of the Royal Academy, and thanks the President and Secretary for "the invariable kindness" with which they have responded to his inquiries for information—such is his authority.

† Mr. Charles Williams stated recently at the Journalists' meeting that the Prince of Wales, a few years ago, declined to attend luncheon at Halifax because the Pressmen were not allowed at the table; and Mr. Peacock added that Mr. Disraeli "shut himself up" in a room on learning of a similar resolve. A gentle reminder of the same sort now from the Prince of Wales and Lord Salisbury would bring the Royal Academy to their senses.

This insult is deeply resented by the Press, some of the principal papers showing their feeling in the matter by boycotting the banquet, and saving much of their valuable space in consequence. Happy thought, I'll do the same!

THE SPIRIT OF FLUNKEYISM

The Soirée Antics.

LL sorts and conditions of men and women crowd the galleries of the Royal Academy on the night set apart for the Soirée late in the season. The exhibitors appear by right, and a medley of somebodies and nobodies are invited by the "President and Council" to meet them.

"*The*" profession is always *the* attraction. Poets and politicians, generals and judges, ambassadors and princes, may come, but "mummer worship" throws all such lights into the shade. That being so, why should not the "mummers" (I use the word in the good old sense, with apologies to Mr. Irving) do something, with their usual generosity, in return? Like all these things, as years roll on vulgarity sets in. The smaller lights take the place of the greater, and burlesque

LOTTIE.

actresses, and even music-hall singers, take the place of the divine
Sarah, the incomparable Ellen, and the beautiful Lillie. No
doubt, if things go on as they appear to be, antics of a choice
nature will run wild. Who knows but, in time to
come, Lotties and Totties and little Bonnies will
come in their stage dress, and then will the High
Art antics of Carrs and Hallés rise in righteous
indignation. At present the President and
Council do little for their guests.
Sir Frederick certainly works hard,
shaking hands or bowing to the
thousands as they pass him. We
see the attendants in red gowns
and fur, we see a few
pots of flowers, and
hear a band play in
the Sculpture Gal-
lery!
   Downstairs,
in the refresh-
ment room,

GUESTS GOING DOWN TO ENJOY THE HOSPITALITY OF THE ROYAL ACADEMY.

surely the hospitality of the Academy will show itself? Their
season is nearly over, their coffers are flowing over with the
shillings of the public. Now is the time to make some return

to the artists who have contributed to the success of their Show,
and to their friends.

Watch the crowd, as I have, going down, anticipating re-
freshments worthy of their host, the Royal Academy of England!
And watch them coming up! the victims of
bitter disappointment, exhausted with the
crush on the stairs, exasperated with the
niggardly provision made for the guests,
hungry and affronted.

The only way to make an Englishman
pleased is to satisfy his
stomach. To rouse him to
anger, try the
other thing. I
firmly believe
this refreshment

GUESTS COMING UP AFTER RECEIVING THE HOSPITALITY OF THE ROYAL ACADEMY.

[NOTE.—I have been too interested in watching the faces of the victims to make a
careful study of the balustrade.—HY. F.]

antic of the Royal Academy does more to injure the reputation
of that mean society than any starving of Art in the eyes of the
great British public.

Few, indeed, of the gushing crowd that by hook or by crook
struggle through the galleries of Burlington House on the night
of the Soirée (or at any other time), have a clear idea of the

object of their visit, save one—that they come to be seen. It is the " thing to do, don't-cher-know," and at that point their interest ceases. To pretend they are doing homage at the shrine of Art is humbug, pure and simple. I repeat, emphatically, the Royal Academy is a *Fashion*—not an *Artistic* influence, but a commercial one ; and once this fact is grasped by Society (with a big " S "), there is an end to Lady Oil's cheap reception.

Contrast it with the Soirée I have seen at the East End

TOTTIE.   BONNIE.

Picture Exhibition. All are welcome, and in their midst stand those interested in something beyond themselves, generously enlightening the visitors with a discourse on the Art around them.

When shall we have the Academy open to the people *free*, as the Salon is ? When shall we have a Soirée given by the Royal Academicians to those who would come in their thousands to *see* and listen—not to be *seen* and gush ?

Never, it seems, until this Mutual Admiration Society—the Royal Academy—is superseded by a National Academy of all arts, for all people.

G

Press Day Antics.

ERHAPS in its peevish treatment of the Press the Royal Academy shows itself, more than in any other way, to be the spoilt, petted child. The over-rated little body cries, " Go away, you nasty Critic ; I don't want you !" The Pen turns away, but the peevish infant pulls at her gown. "Oh! I didn't mean that. I only snub you because you make so much of me, you know ; and I didn't think you would take me at my word."

LITTLE LADY OIL, THE SPOILT CHILD.

We are certainly not proud of our Royal Academy, nor very boastful of our National Gallery, and politics and society may sometimes make us blush ; but we are rightly proud of our newspaper press. No other country in the world can compare with ours for the freedom and excellent tone of our newspapers. Our critics are not bought and sold, as they are in other countries, but artistically and honestly do their work. Nevertheless the Royal Academy treats the Press with marked contempt. It is with difficulty Press-tickets are obtained. Red-tapeism arm-in-arm with flunkeyism is rampant at Burlington House.

My readers will hardly credit the fact that the proprietor of our aristocratic daily paper, himself a leader of society, applied for a Press-ticket, so that he might accompany his art critic, and was refused, as " one ticket had already been sent to the paper." A paper, mark you, which circulates among the class the Royal Academicians go down to on their knees!

A member of the Press is first reminded of Royal Academy parsimony on presenting his invitation at the doors, where the official savagely shears a corner off the card, and—would you credit it?—holds the fragment as a receipt for the catalogue, value two pence! Should it be lost, you may ask in vain for another, and, of course, your solitary day for the pictures is practically lost. No; the official is not allowed to sell a copy. Bah! down with this vexatious stupidity! Come, Lady Oil, treat the critics you invite to your house like gentlemen, and not like area sneaks! This one-catalogue nuisance is not the case at other art exhibitions, and I must say I have never seen a critic exhibit any kleptomaniac tendencies in consequence.

The first thing to strike you on entering the galleries (as soon as you have recovered from the insult of your honesty being doubted by having your ticket mutilated) is that the floors are freshly waxed, and the unfortunate critic is in jeopardy of coming to grief. Is there any deep-rooted design in this to put an end to art-critics? A little more wax and their fate would be sealed—they would break their necks. "No, better finish them off by overwork," thinks my Lady Oil. "We hang over 2,000 works, and only give the 'paper fellows' nine hours to study, mark, learn, and inwardly digest the lot. Ha! ha! how I gloat over their sufferings! For poor ink-slingers have to live. And don't we cry out if the poor dazed overworked scribblers make a slip! Bless you, they must, with over 2,000 works, and only one day to themselves: and that often a dark, wet, or foggy one." See here is a cry from *Truth's* "young man":—

PITY THE POOR ART-CRITIC.—A time of trial is approaching for the much-abused fraternity of which I am a humble member. In a week we shall be turned loose in the

ONLY A CRITIC !

Academy — turned loose for the space of a single day among 2,000 pictures, drawings, engravings, and sculptures ; and woe be unto us if in the space of that day we are unable to give a more or less accurate description of every notable work of art which adorns or disfigures the walls of Burlington House. *Sic vos non vobis* is or ought to be our motto, but never do we so entirely justify its truth as on the Press day of the Royal Academy Exhibition. Few of my readers, I imagine, have ever assisted at this function ; let me describe it. Last year, to be precise, there were 1,052 oil paintings ; 361 water-colours and miniatures; 169 etchings, drawings, and engravings; 198 architectural drawings; and 166 pieces of sculpture : grand total, 1,946. This year, I presume, the numbers will certainly not be less. Now, I want to know how any mortal man or woman can be expected to work through this enormous mass of material in six hours? Six days would not be too long. Mr. Harry Furniss wrote on the subject last year, and demanded a week.* I will be more moderate, but I most emphatically assert that no man can "do" the Academy properly in less than three days. Guileless outsiders may say, "You can come back later." Quite so, but for the first three or four weeks

"Here we are again."   "That's one gallery I've seen."   "The fourth."   "Five o'clock. I'll never get through."   "I may do it yet."   "No. A fog! and still one thousand works to study."

THAT'S HOW IT'S DONE BY THE ART-CRITIC.

the rooms are so crammed that it is impossible to study a picture, and difficult even to see it. And this brings me to another grievance. The Academy is the only great gallery in London to which the art-critic is denied free entry during the season. It is not a question of money. Art-critics can generally scrape together five shillings for a season ticket, or at all events their editors are, as a rule, sufficiently well off to afford the unprofitable outlay. It is a question of common civility. Why, I ask,

* "A Growl at the R.A.," my letter to the *Daily News*, May 17th, 1887.

should editors gratuitously puff the private show of the R.A.'s —for, of course, we have suppressed long ago all that nonsense about the Academy being a national exhibition —in many columns of their journals, when even this poor compliment is boorishly withheld from them or their representatives? The leading papers are not so hard up for "copy" that they could not afford to ignore the Academy altogether. I should very much like to see the effect upon the R.A.'s—those grotesquely self-satisfied Olympians— of a conspiracy of silence on the part of even half-a-dozen leading London newspapers! But this is by no means all. The Academy is open to the critics at the end of April or very early in May. More often than not an east wind is raging, a blizzard storms along Piccadilly, or a cold sleety rain pours from a leaden sky. The damp and shivering critic betakes himself at an untimely hour to Burlington House, and is received by a surly attendant, who grudgingly hands him a catalogue, and as a favour takes charge of his umbrella. Scattered through the great empty galleries are two score more or so shivering mortals bent on the same errand. The rooms are not warmed; the attendant tells you, "The weather is so uncertain; they did not think it would be cold;" the refreshment-room is shut; you may not smoke. I once did, but the *genius loci* overcame me, and I hid my cigarette in terror. Now, I have not the slightest desire to revel at the expense of the R.A.'s in chicken and champagne. My wants are much more simple. I cannot support nature from 10 a.m. to 5 or 6 p.m. on nothing, and a sandwich and a glass of sherry would "assuage the pangs," as Mrs. Gamp remarked, and would also save me the annoyance of voyaging out to a restaurant or a club in search of sustenance. I do not ask for sesquipedalian cigars of 1881 tobacco, but I think that the R.A.'s might afford us a few cigarettes—you can buy quite smokable cigarettes for seven shillings per 100. As for the neglect to warm the vast bleak galleries, it is simply barbarous and brutal.

My wants, therefore, I sum up in a few words. Three days at least wherein to see the pictures, instead of one; a modest expenditure of coal; a glass of sherry and a sandwich; a cigarette, or at least liberty to smoke one; and a season ticket. I may say at once that if the first boon be granted I will cheerfully forego the rest, and I appeal to my brethren of the Press to make their voices heard, and heard emphatically, on this subject. Mr. Harry Furniss wrote, as I have said, vigorously last year. I wish he would get up a round-robin for presentation to the Academicians; for it must be a very emphatic and united protest which would have the smallest effect upon the obtuse sensibilities of the gentry who sit beside their nectar drawing in the multitudinous shillings of the British public—careless of the woes of frozen, wearied, and hungry art-critics.

The writer makes one mistake in this admirable description of Press day. I did not ask for a week; I wrote, "Why not put aside three clear days for the art-critics, and allow an enterprising old applewoman to start a stall in the building, to provide some sort of refreshment? . . . The refreshment rooms are closed; so if one forgets to pocket a biscuit before leaving home, he loses most valuable time in rushing to his club to avoid fainting from hunger before getting half through the usual exhibition of dazzling ability. Last Press day I saw one most eminent journalist retire into the Sculpture Room, and then nervously eat sandwiches he had brought with him and, when the door-keeper's eye was turned, sip sherry-and-water from a travelling flask. I offer this incident to any Royal Academician in want of an historical subject."

I may supplement these remarks of mine by asking my Lady Oil, Does she or does she not wish the critics to see the pictures and sculpture? If she does, and will not allow the hungry critic to beg, borrow, or steal any decent lunch, why not the old applewoman? A hurried morsel to "assuage the pangs," and a bottle of ginger-beer, and then on with the critic's

WHICH IS IT TO BE?

wild career. But if her ladyship's object is *not* to allow the critic to see the 2,000 works, then I offer a suggestion, more artistic and pleasing than her present starvation scheme, which, like the freezing one, is "simply barbarous and brutal."

If her ladyship ever condescends to walk across Piccadilly to her wronged sister Water-Colour, she will see the pretty attendants there, serving afternoon tea. *Verb. sap!* Here is a scene on Press day as it might be, and I'll guarantee the pictures would never be criticised, except of course by Mr. Punch and the writer.

It is curious to note the extraordinary people who turn up on Press day. Some unaccountable antic of Mr. Red Tape, who refuses admission to the proprietor of a leading London paper, and admits old ladies, young girls, school-boys, curates, and other mixtures ; where they come from, and what they write for, is a mystery. Soon we will have the youthful representative of the other sex, as lady journalists are coming to the fore. Indeed, the number of ladies on Press day is on the increase, and some of

ONE OF THE PRIVILEGED FEW.

the best criticisms come from their pens. Yet even the ladies are treated in the same "barbarous and brutal" manner as their brother-critics.

It is an understood thing, of course, R.A.'s and A.R.A.'s keep away on Press day, and leave their Show to the critics ; but I have noticed one of the young R.A.'s present on Press day, lately (not far from his own picture). I may tell him he has no right there; it is the critics' day. If his want of taste prompts him to think otherwise, then let the "lady-killer" act as any other gentleman would, and look after the comforts of the ladies at least, by offering them sherry and biscuit, or afternoon tea.

Mr. M. H. Spielmann, one of the keenest and kindest of

A CRITIC OF THE FUTURE.

art-critics, in his admirable address in defence of his craft, delivered at the Edinburgh Art Congress last year, said :—

"If artists really care about the condition of our art-criticism, and desire to see in the critic, so far as they are concerned, something more than a mere gratuitous advertisement agent, they cannot—they must not—be backward in this matter. I believe that if facilities were given by the throwing open of studios, the critic would take advantage of them, watching the artist while his work was in progress, and while becoming familiar with the executive portion of his art, would ascertain his aims more thoroughly, and his artistic code of morality far better, than he could learn them from the artist's exhibited work. In this manner a better knowledge of each other would spring up, and a truer sympathy for each other's work would be developed. No longer would the critic be chargeable, as Mr. Hodgson expresses it, with 'viewing the scenic displays of art from his place in the stalls or boxes.' The position of the critic would probably become more difficult in consequence of the friendships that would certainly grow up, but I believe that his practised moral courage, fostered by the nature of his work, would enable him to rise superior to all temptation."

Very pretty, Mr. Spielmann, but is such a thing possible ? Picture to yourself the unfortunate painter in a mess with his picture, harassed by a stupid model, depressed by an exacting dealer, worried by wife and domestics, cursed by our foggy climate, having the moral courage " to rise superior to all temptation " to use a great big D, and calmly welcome, at such a moment, critics to sit around him, note-book in hand, and "in consequence of the friendship that would certainly grow up," probably smoking cigars, and sipping afternoon tea. Why, the eagle eye of Mr. Spielmann alone would suffice to drive all working power out of the nervous artist, to say nothing of the chattering verbosity of your artist-critic, or the rampant heckling of the lady writer. And then would not the "ghosts" be seen, and the "tricks" disclosed ? Where would Turner's reputation have been had Ruskin seen the great master use water-colour for the skies in his oil pictures, and cut out figures in paper, and stick them on his masterpieces ? Yet, if I am rightly informed, some of the finest works of Turner in our National Gallery are mixtures of oil and water, and scissors and paste.

I fail to see what charge Mr. Hodgson brings against the critic. Surely the proper place to view scenic displays is from the stalls and boxes ? In the scene-painter's garret you can discern nothing. I would rather remind Mr. Hodgson and his fellow Academicians that whereas theatrical scenic work is shown to the greatest advantage, in the very place and in the very light intended by the artist, so that perspective and effect is seen to perfection, pictures painted in the studio for the line in the Academy, and worthy of the place, are frequently "skied" in a bad light, or, worse still, ruthlessly ruined by being hung between pictures that do not harmonise, and therefore kill all the effect intended by the painter. For this reason I agree with Mr. Spielmann that art-critics ought to see pictures before they leave the studio.

A happy thought has struck me. Why should not art-critics disguise themselves, and visit the studios whilst the pictures are in progress? Mr. Spielmann with a false beard would be welcomed as a millionaire, Mr. Humphry Ward in High Church clerical garb, and Mr. Andrew Lang in his golfing get-up.

It has become the fashion for artists to pooh - pooh art-criticism. Mr. Frith leads the opposition in the name of the old Academicians, and Professor Richmond for the younger members. I will close this chapter by quoting my remarks * à propos of Mr. Frith's startling charge. He says :—

" I would advise all artists, young and old, never to read art-criticism. Nothing is to be learnt from it."

Now, notwithstanding this genial artist's sweeping condemnation of the Press, I venture to assert the friend in need is the art-critic. He encourages the young artist, instructs him, and when he has come to his seventh stage, gently gives him the hint to retire.

The pen is mightier than the sword, so the sword objects to it. It therefore follows the leaden-headed pencil should squeak with even greater ferocity.

The pen is the pencil's best friend. The pen of Ruskin made known the pencil of Turner, and why, in this sense, should not every critic be a Ruskin, every painter a Turner? We in art owe to the Press to-day a debt of gratitude that can never be repaid, for educating the public in matters of art. Artists' pictures are often only the texts for writers' sermons.

And although genius like that of Mr. Orchardson (whom I venture to call the Thackeray of the brush) writes its own sermons in his admirable pictures, or Mr. Alma-Tadema's (whose technique in painting travels hand-in-hand with the thought and study in his work)—although such exceptional genius may assert itself without advertisement, in most cases the critic is the cement which keeps the body of painters and the public together. And if a National Academy of Arts, as I propose, is to become a reality, it is free criticism, which has already laid its foundation stone, that must build it up bit by bit, carting away

* Lecture, " Art and Artists."

the rubbish dug out of the hot-bed of prejudice, and eventually throw open to all a National Temple of Art, worthily representing in each of its various forms all the artistic talent of this great country.

The Seven Ages of the Royal Academician, and his Antics.

OW sad it is to see men whose work we may have admired continue to paint until our children laugh at their senile efforts!

Sans touch, *sans* eyes, *sans* colour, *sans* everything. But he sticks to his colours like an old soldier, and parades his line pictures in the same large space they have occupied for years.

Again I quote the Academician who lately has unburdened his soul to us. He says :—

"Very few indeed are the examples of painters' powers remaining unshaken by time. If, as Shakespeare says, 'Time cannot wither (certain things), nor custom stale their infinite variety,' the observation will not apply to my profession, and one of the knottiest problems left for Academic solution at the present time is that of reconciling prescriptive rights with the interests of Art, and the interests of the painters themselves. Everybody knows the story of Gil Blas and the Bishop of

Granada. Nature kindly, or unkindly, hides from a man the knowledge of his failing powers. How often do I hear old painters say, on 'showing a mere shadow of a shade' of former power, 'There, I mean to say I never painted a better picture in my life than that!' I have no doubt I shall soon be using similar language, and when I do, I hope I shall find a friend to act the part of Gil Blas for me, when I promise not to imitate the Bishop of Granada."

What does the " Grand Old Man of Art "—Mr. G. F. Watts —say ?—

" In my seventy-fourth year I cannot be certain of being up to my old level, and I have asked for severe judgment from the council of selection and the hanging committee, in order to be sure of not disgracing the Academy and myself—so I may have nothing there. Of course, it is probable that the council may find my contribution sufficiently satisfactory to hang, but I am very sincere in my desire to have my work judged even severely. We have seen deplorable examples of failure of eye and hand, and I much desire not to be added to the number."

Good, noble sentiments from both. But why should such confession be necessary ? * If a man cannot serve his country as a soldier for more than seven years, is it possible he can serve his country in art without preventing—in a limited body— rising talent from having a chance ? Sir Edwin Landseer said, " A man's hand or head does not last more than twenty-five years, and therefore the time arrives in one's career when the fewer pictures one sends the better."

By the death of Mr. Herbert the Royal Academy loses its rarest specimen of the seventh age. But others are swiftly slipping from the sixth; and is it not too dreadful to contemplate that soon we shall have " deplorable examples of failure of eye and hand " to disgrace our country's art under the wing of Incompetency, the Royal Academy ?

How can I better explain this headline than by the designs for seven cartoons illustrating the subject, which I'll ask you to believe are drawn by a Royal Academician in his seventh age ?

* See also Sir Thomas Lawrence's, page 31.

THE FIRST AGE.

First the baby daubing in its nurse's arms.   Observe delight of fond parent coming down the studio stairs, and the aged grandma, who brings the youthful genius his first box of paints, held by the page-boy.

The subject of the picture on the easel is the " Infancy of Art."

THE SECOND AGE.

And then the artist school-boy, with his irrepressible genius coming to the surface. Observe the weeping mother, and the finely-pointed moral in the left-hand corner.

THE THIRD AGE.

Sighing like furnace, with a woeful ballad made to his mistress's eyebrow.

Fail not to note the neglected picture on the easel ; the eyebrows only have as
yet been painted. In the middle distance we see the object of his affections, and her
fat poodle—a sad contrast to the half-starved favourites of the painter. Truly a stroke
of genius worthy of a Hogarth, to note the fact that youths in love cannot eat, and
their selfishness leads them to forget the bones for their canine friends. Observe the
angry father in the distance, his three acres and a cow, and the rustic dove-cot.

THE FOURTH AGE.

Seeking a bubble reputation even in the cannon's mouth.

NOTE.—It is easy to follow this interesting picture-drama. Cut by the wouldn't-be father-in-law, the artist recklessly flies away to seek fame and fortune.

So conscientious is he in his work, he fails to observe that his eyebrowed lady-love has followed him, and is acting the part of a Florence Nightingale : she is supporting a wounded drummer-boy, who dies with the portrait of his mother in his hand—a truly original conception. I am not quite sure if that circle in the air represents a cannon ball or the bubble reputation ; but the master is rightly proud of the easy manner in which he conveys the idea of a regiment of soldiers in the left-hand corner ; the spear-heads are a satire on the manufacture of British bayonets and swords, and the horse, which some might consider under-sized, is true to nature, a native pony accustomed to jump from hill-top to hill-top at least, the master has written a note to that effect on the back of this stirring design.

THE FIFTH AGE.

Then the full Academician, with vest well lined, full of wise saws and modern pictures (probably accounts for his pained expression), and so he blows his own trumpet. Surrounded by his pupils, he discourses upon the portrait of his wife (begun in Age Three), and is prepared to meet the shiploads of foreign artists who are coming to England to sit on the steps of the Royal Academy.

THE SIXTH AGE.

The lean and slippered pantaloon.

The full Academician, still older, having passed his life in turning out pictures with the greatest rapidity, now takes a keen delight in turning out the works of others with even greater rapidity.

THE SEVENTH AGE.

Last scene of all that ends this strange eventful history, sans touch, sans eyes, sans colour, sans everything but canvas, with only one pupil left.

Nursed by the eyebrowed wife, who keeps all criticism from him, he starts his Academy pictures. Note the arrival of fresh canvases, which are doubtless for portraits, and the exceedingly interesting and well-drawn surroundings.

Personal.

I am well aware that members of the Royal Academy pretend that the words of "a caricaturist" are heeded not, but I would humbly remind those Royal Academicians that I have lectured to many thousands of their intelligent countrymen, and my suggestions for a National Academy have been at all places received in a manner clearly showing that truths, even—nay, *especially when*—coming from a caricaturist, must sooner or later open the eyes of the public to see the hollowness of the Burlington House idol, and its injustice to national art.

Furthermore, the Press all over the country has spoken out pretty freely in support of my claim for reform, and supported me in every particular.

Most of those artists who write and talk of Art may be considered prejudiced; no one can well say that I am. What is the Royal Academy to me?

I assume the reader knows the good that is always claimed --and not without justice—on behalf of the Academy and its influence; more than that, I assume that you have never heard anything but good of the Academy and its careful fostering of Art.

AND THAT IS WHY IN THIS LITTLE VOLUME I THINK IT SUFFICIENT, FOR THE SAKE OF JUSTICE TO ART, AND TO THOSE ARTISTS WHO FOR ONE REASON OR ANOTHER ARE NOT WITHIN THE INNER CIRCLE, TO CALL YOUR DISCRIMI-NATING ATTENTION TO THE EVIL THE ACADEMY WORKS AND PERMITS TO EXIST.

The Academician is in reality a member of a very exclusive club, and nothing more. That is not generally understood by the public. It imagines the artist is elected to rule, and do good to Art in the country.

If being a member of a gigantic sale-room, with the privilege of having the best space to show his own wares, and a sort of Hall-stamp " R.A.," so that he can raise the price of those wares, is being a benefactor to Art, then I've nothing further to say. It is a fashion ; not an artistic influence, but a commercial one, and if the body will frankly acknowledge this fact, they of course may, in a purely commercial spirit, claim the right to do as they like with their own.

Unquestionably when the Academy was founded, Art in this country, with one or two brilliant exceptions, was at a very low ebb, and the Academy as thus constituted doubtless fulfilled all its requirements.

But the sea of talent has since risen rapidly and now beats against the walls of Burlington House.

Let us think of the injustice as matters stand at present.

Painters in oil, sculptors, architects, and engravers are alone eligible as candidates.

I have pointed out before the absurdity of electing architects and engravers, and excluding painters in water-colours and artists in black and white. The injustice is too glaring to require comment. I see no reason why all should not be elected. Why this invidious distinction and favouritism ?

I propose a National Academy, a Commonwealth of Art, presided over by a State Minister of Fine Art, in which mediocrity will find no space till a welcome and a place have been given to all earnest work, regardless of its nature.

Where the number of works of any one man will be limited, and where there will be no such mockery of good work as "rejection for want of space."

Where all the fine arts, and especially the national fine art (water-colour painting), shall be recognised as arts, and the best of the professors of them shall at least be eligible for election.

Where the committee of selection and hanging shall be— as in the Salon—elected by the body of the exhibitors.

Where reasonable time is given to the proper consideration of every work sent in.

Where women, in the rare event of their being equal to their brother brushes, shall be elected into the magic circle.

These improvements have been mostly urged upon the consideration of the Academy of late, as you are probably aware. But notwithstanding the efforts of many right-minded members of their body, the majority adopt the Fabian policy of sitting down and doing nothing, or bury their heads, ostrich-like, till the storm of indignation raised by their unworthy selfishness and indolence has blown over.

The evidence before the Select Committee on Arts, 1836, proves conclusively that, in the opinion of many, private academic institutions connected with the arts—the Royal Academy, in particular—are a mistake. It was pretty clearly shown that in place of being Art's foster-mother it was the Upas tree, under whose branches genius was stifled and rancour engendered. This poor tree was sadly blown about by stormy winds at the time, many of its branches which were rotten snapped off, while the others grated against each other in noisy discord. Unpopularity enveloped it in clouds of dust then, as it does now. When the exhibition time came round, and gate money was in view, saplings from the outside forest of talent were grafted on to its trunk, soon to be torn away again.

But the insect of selfishness has begun its work. These

storms come and go with the season ; the old tree, still quivering,
is propped up by ignorant fashionable patronage. But well it
knows that the insect's work is fatal, and that the storm of
indignation growing stronger—now on the horizon—will sooner
or later sweep down in tremendous fury, and the tree planted by
the deluded king in the secrecy of night will be rooted up,
and leave exposed to public view at last its corrupted core.
Then the ground will be ploughed over, and the soil tilled ; and
we shall have, in place of this present narrow clique, a National
Academy of Art, with a fair field and no favour !

A few Cards from the Press and others

Left at the Door of the Royal Academy.

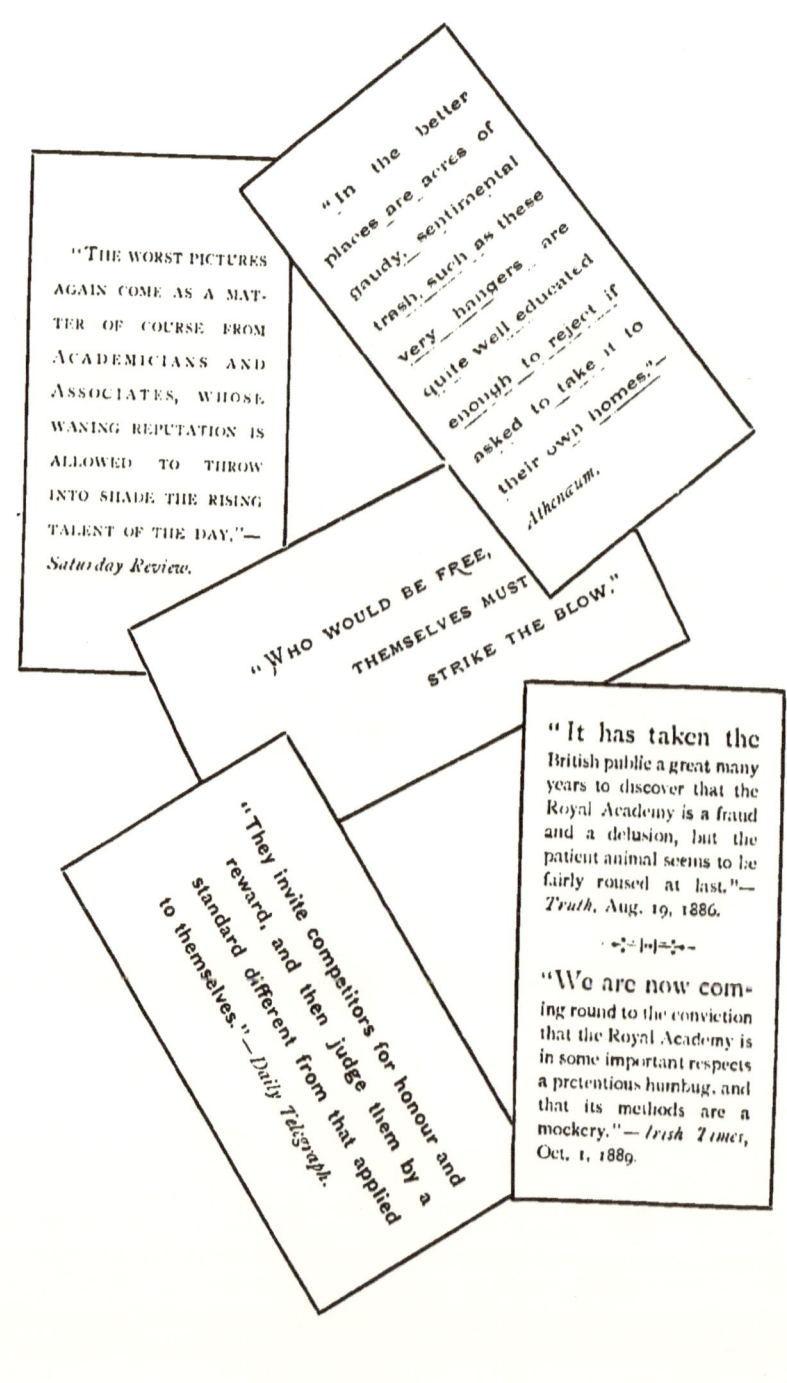

"THE WORST PICTURES AGAIN COME AS A MATTER OF COURSE FROM ACADEMICIANS AND ASSOCIATES, WHOSE WANING REPUTATION IS ALLOWED TO THROW INTO SHADE THE RISING TALENT OF THE DAY."— *Saturday Review.*

"In the better places are acres of gaudy, sentimental trash, such as these very hangers are quite well educated enough to reject if asked to take it to their own homes." *Athenæum.*

"WHO WOULD BE FREE, THEMSELVES MUST STRIKE THE BLOW."

"They invite competitors for honour and reward, and then judge them by a standard different from that applied to themselves."—*Daily Telegraph.*

"It has taken the British public a great many years to discover that the Royal Academy is a fraud and a delusion, but the patient animal seems to be fairly roused at last."— *Truth*, Aug. 19, 1886.

"We are now coming round to the conviction that the Royal Academy is in some important respects a pretentious humbug, and that its methods are a mockery."—*Irish Times,* Oct. 1, 1889.

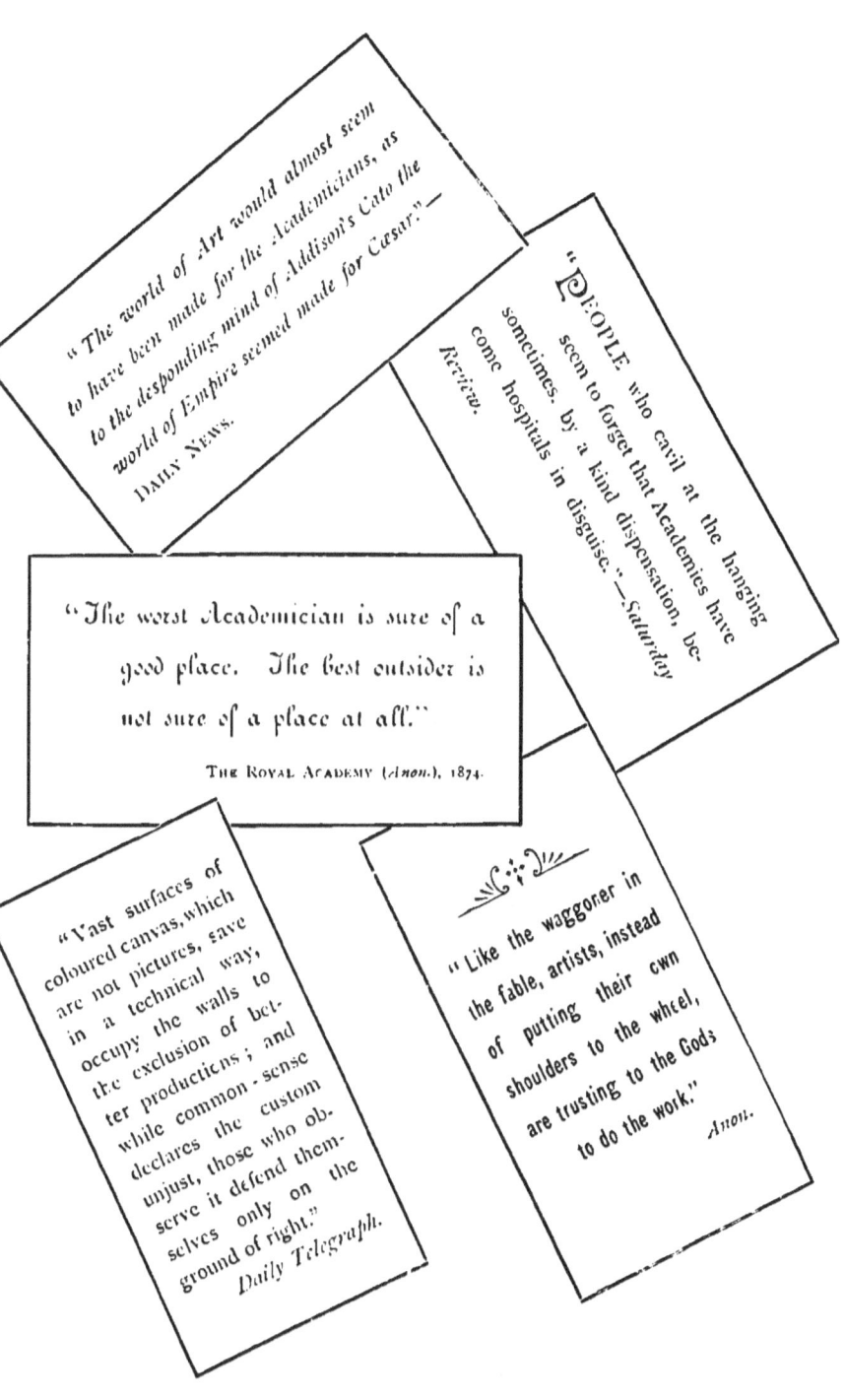

"The world of Art would almost seem to have been made for the Academicians, as to the desponding mind of Addison's Cato the world of Empire seemed made for Cæsar."—DAILY NEWS.

"PEOPLE who cavil at the hanging seem to forget that Academies have sometimes, by a kind dispensation, become hospitals in disguise."—Saturday Review.

"The worst Academician is sure of a good place. The best outsider is not sure of a place at all."

THE ROYAL ACADEMY (Anon.), 1874.

"Vast surfaces of coloured canvas, which are not pictures, save in a technical way, occupy the walls to the exclusion of better productions; and while common-sense declares the custom unjust, those who observe it defend themselves only on the ground of right."
Daily Telegraph.

"Like the waggoner in the fable, artists, instead of putting their own shoulders to the wheel, are trusting to the Gods to do the work."

Anon.

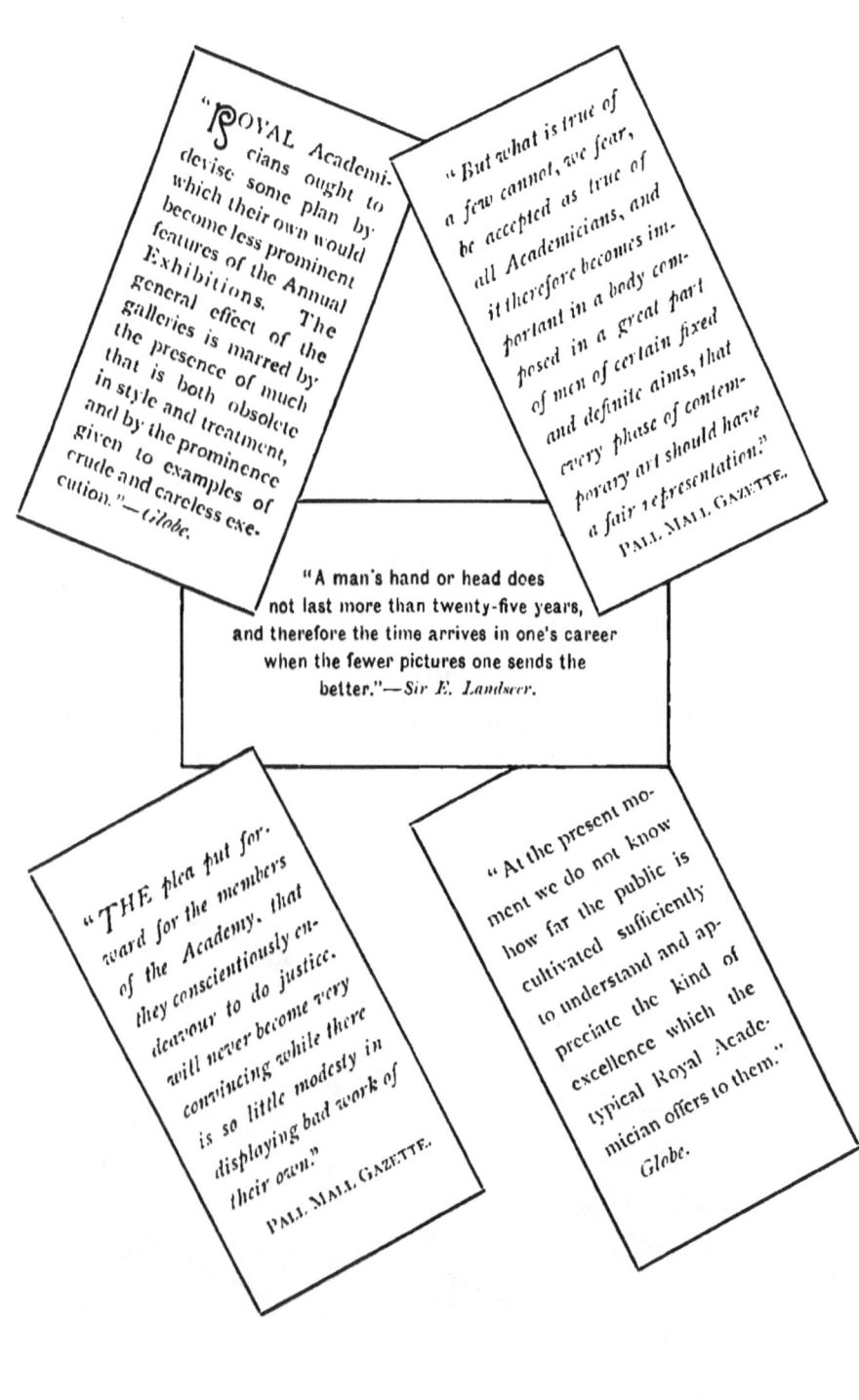

"ROYAL Academicians ought to devise some plan by which their own would become less prominent features of the Annual Exhibitions. The general effect of the galleries is marred by the presence of much that is both obsolete in style and treatment, and by the prominence given to examples of crude and careless execution."—*Globe.*

"But what is true of a few cannot, we fear, be accepted as true of all Academicians, and it therefore becomes important in a body composed in a great part of men of certain fixed and definite aims, that every phase of contemporary art should have a fair representation." PALL MALL GAZETTE.

"A man's hand or head does not last more than twenty-five years, and therefore the time arrives in one's career when the fewer pictures one sends the better."—*Sir E. Landseer.*

"THE plea put forward for the members of the Academy, that they conscientiously endeavour to do justice, will never become very convincing while there is so little modesty in displaying bad work of their own." PALL MALL GAZETTE.

"At the present moment we do not know how far the public is cultivated sufficiently to understand and appreciate the kind of excellence which the typical Royal Academician offers to them." *Globe.*

INDEX.

THE END.

PRINTED BY CASSELL & COMPANY, LIMITED, LA BELLE SAUVAGE, LONDON, E.C.
20.590

HARRY FURNISS'S
ROYAL ACADEMY.

AN ARTISTIC JOKE.

HE Exhibition consisted of eighty-seven pictures, in black and white of course, but otherwise similar in size and general appearance to those annually seen on the walls of Burlington House. Anyone who visited it must have seen that it was the result of many years of labour, and not a few of the pictures possessed an artistic value quite apart from their interest as pictorial travesties. A wish has been very generally expressed that some permanent record, in a portable shape, but in character consonant with the artistic purpose of the Exhibition, should be procurable by the public at large, both those who saw and those who did not see the originals at the Gainsborough Gallery and elsewhere.

To meet this wish an **ALBUM**, containing Reproductions of these **EIGHTY-SEVEN PICTURES**, with which will be included the contents of **THE ILLUSTRATED CATALOGUE**, has been prepared and largely subscribed for. The issue of these Albums, however, which will be the only reproductions of the Exhibition, is strictly limited to **ONE THOUSAND COPIES**, each of which will be signed by the Artist.

It may be mentioned that the whole of this undertaking, from its conception to the present time, has been in Mr. Furniss's own hand. This has enabled Mr. Furniss scrupulously to maintain the artistic character of the whole enterprise. In the preparation of this Album he has spared no time or expense in trying reproductions by the different processes at home and abroad, similar to those used in the Album of the Royal Academy Pictures of 1886, and the annual reproductions of the French Salon. Not, however, being satisfied with any of these cheaper methods, he has, regardless of the great cost, adopted the finest method of photogravure viz., the Photo Intaglio process of A. and C. Dawson, No. 3, Farringdon Street, and Hogarth Works, Chiswick, the reproductions being made under his own supervision. Each plate is hand-printed, and will in every way surpass, for artistic quality, anything of the kind ever published.

As PHOTOGRAVURE is the best and most faithful, as well as the most expensive method, this Album is certain to be valuable, and a worthy and competent memorial of the "Artistic Joke"; whilst the price charged will be only £3 3s., the same as fixed, originally, when the adoption of the cheaper process was contemplated.

The size of the Album is Imperial Quarto (11 by 15 inches) ; the plates range, on an average, from 4 × 6 to 7½ × 9 inches. The whole is handsomely and tastefully bound in cloth and gilt edged.

AFTER THE THOUSAND VERITABLE *Édition de luxe* WERE PRINTED, THE PLATES WERE DESTROYED.

The whole Edition is rapidly being exhausted, and the price will be raised to **FIVE Guineas** shortly.

Orders should be forwarded to THE TYPOGRAPHIC-ETCHING Co., No. 3, Farringdon Street. £3 3s. 6d. (including Case for packing).

An ETCHING or PHOTOGRAVURE

IS NOW GIVEN IN EACH PART OF

THE MAGAZINE OF ART.

Monthly, price One Shilling.

"The Magazine of Art contains a very storehouse of Art. The illustrations are numerous ; the letterpress is particularly good and varied, being designed to suit all tastes, from the most to the least artistic. . . Every year The Magazine of Art more surely justifies its name, both by the quality of its illustrations and its letterpress."— *The Times.*

"The exquisite beauty of the engravings in The Magazine of Art, and the excellence of the letterpress, should carry the magazine into every home where Art is appreciated." — *Standard.*

"The Magazine of Art is far superior to any artistic serial ever produced for a shilling."— *Daily Chronicle.*

"The best written and best illustrated of the Art periodicals—a wonderful shilling's-worth." *The Graphic.*

"The Magazine of Art represents Art and the artistic movements of the day better than any other periodical."—*Saturday Review.*

" Every sort of fine or decorative art is represented in The Magazine of Art. Its literary excellence is certainly not less than its artistic grace."—*Spectator.*

"The Magazine of Art contains better literature, it seems to us, than any of the other Art periodicals." -*Pall Mall Gazette.*

'The only Art magazine which at all keeps pace with the moving current of Art." *Academy.*

"The exquisite illustrations are not equalled in any other magazine." —*Manchester Examiner.*

CASSELL & COMPANY, Limited *La Belle Sauvage, Ludgate Hill, London,*

"Royal Academy Pictures,"

1890.

In THREE PARTS, ONE SHILLING each.

EXTRACT FROM PROSPECTUS.

The Proprietors of THE MAGAZINE OF ART have the pleasure to announce that a further development will mark the publication of ROYAL ACADEMY PICTURES for **1890**.

The first issue (1888), which consisted of a single Part, at once achieved a remarkable popularity. Last year the work was published in Two Parts, so as to give a more adequate representation of the contents of the Academy, and a greatly increased circulation resulted. Many important pictures had nevertheless to be omitted, and this year it has been determined to issue the work in **Three Parts** at **1s.** each, that full justice may be done to the Exhibition.

The Three Parts will contain upwards of ONE HUNDRED beautiful reproductions of representative pictures of the Academy, and will form a comprehensive and permanent fine-art record of this year's Exhibition.

The following selections from the reviews of last year's issue will be of interest.

" The beautifully printed pictures will delight visitors to the Academy and be a source of abiding interest to those who may be kept away."—*Daily Chronicle.*

" It is really much more sensible to pay for and possess such a souvenir of the Academy than to pay for the doubtful privilege of being crowded and jostled into discomfort in the rather hopeless attempt to see the pictures themselves at Burlington House."—*Weekly Times.*

" No one having the least taste for pictures, aware of the existence of this work, would be without a copy. We say advisedly that any one of the reproductions is worth much more than the charge for the whole."—*Malvern Advertiser.*

⁎⁎It may be stated that ROYAL ACADEMY PICTURES FOR 1888 *has been advanced in price from* 1s. *to* 1s. 6d. *Part* 1 *of the* 1889 *Edition, though advanced to* 2s. 6d., *is now entirely out of print. Copies of Part* 2 *only can now be had, and the price of this will be raised in due course.*

CASSELL & COMPANY, LIMITED, Ludgate Hill, London ; and all Booksellers.

FINE ART VOLUMES

Published by CASSELL & COMPANY.

The Rivers of Great Britain : Descriptive, Historical, Pictorial. RIVERS OF THE EAST COAST, with numerous highly finished Engravings. Royal 4to, 384 pages, cloth gilt, gilt edges, with Etching as Frontispiece, price 42s.

The Royal River : The Thames from Source to Sea. With Descriptive Text by the Rev. T. G. BONNEY, D.Sc., LL.D., J. RUNCIMAN, W. SENIOR, H. SCHÜTZ WILSON, GODFREY TURNER, AARON WATSON, &c., and a Series of Beautiful Engravings from Original Designs by Leading Artists. Cloth gilt, £2 2s.

The International Shakspere. Consisting of an *Edition de luxe* of the Principal Plays of Shakspere, with Illustrations by the Leading Artists of the World, produced in the highest style of Photogravure.

    AS YOU LIKE IT. Illustrated by M, ÉMILE BAYARD. 70s.

    KING HENRY IV. Illustrated by Herr EDUARD GRÜTZNER. 70s.

    "ROMEO AND JULIET" was issued at 70s., but the growing scarcity of copies compelled the Publishers to advance the price to £5 5s.

    THREE SERIES, price One Guinea each.

Character Sketches from Dickens. Each containing SIX ORIGINAL DRAWINGS by FREDERICK BARNARD. Reproduced in Photogravure. Size 20 by 14½ inches. In Portfolio.

Character Sketches from Thackeray. Six New and Original Drawings by FREDERICK BARNARD, reproduced in Photogravure, on India Paper. Size 20 by 14½ inches. In Portfolio, price 21s.

Egypt : Descriptive, Historical, and Picturesque. By Prof. G. EBERS. Translated by CLARA BELL, with Notes by SAMUEL BIRCH, LL.D., D.C.L., F.S.A. Complete in Two Handsome Volumes. With about 800 Original Engravings. *Popular Edition.* Two Vols., 42s.

The Magazine of Art. Yearly Volume for 1889. Vol. XII. With 12 Exquisite Etchings, Photogravures, &c., and several Hundred choice Engravings from Original Drawings and from famous Paintings. Cloth, 16s.

Picturesque Canada : A Delineation by Pen and Pencil of all the Features of Interest in the Dominion of Canada, from its Discovery to the Present Day. With about 600 Original Illustrations. Complete in Two Volumes, £3 3s. each.

Picturesque Europe. Complete in Five Volumes. Each containing Thirteen Exquisite Steel Plates from Original Drawings, and nearly 200 Original Illustrations drawn on Wood by some of the First Artists of the Day. *Popular Edition,* Five Vols., 18s. each.

    Vols. I. and II., comprising the BRITISH ISLES, can also be had bound together. Cloth gilt, 31s. 6d.

    . *A few copies of the* ORIGINAL LARGE QUARTO EDITION, *complete in Five Volumes, cloth gilt, gilt edges, £21, or morocco, £52 10s., can still be obtained, in Sets only.*

Picturesque America. Complete in Four Volumes, with Twelve Exquisite Steel Plates and about 200 Original Wood Engravings in each. Royal 4to, handsomely bound in cloth gilt, gilt edges, £2 2s. each.

Abbeys and Churches of England and Wales. Descriptive, Historical, Pictorial. With Original Illustrations by Eminent Artists. Edited by Rev. Prof. BONNEY, F.R.S. 21s.

Longfellow's Poetical Works. Fine-Art Edition. Illustrated throughout with Original Engravings. Royal 4to, cloth gilt, £3 3s. *Popular Edition.* Extra crown 4to, cloth gilt, 16s.

Illustrated History of Music. By EMIL NAUMANN, Director of Music at the Chapel Royal Dresden, and Translated by FERDINAND PRAEGER. Revised and Edited by the late Rev. Sir F. A. GORE OUSELEY, Bart., Mus. Doc. With Authentic Illustrations. Two Vols., 31s. 6d.

CASSELL & COMPANY, LIMITED, *London, Paris & Melbourne.*

PRACTICAL ART MANUALS.

With numerous COLOURED PLATES *in each.*

Marine Painting. By WALTER W. MAY, R.I. 5s.

Flowers, and How to Paint Them. By MAUD NAFTEL. 5s.

Sepia Painting, A Course of. Two Volumes. 3s. each. Also in one Volume, 5s.

Animal Painting in Water Colours. By FREDERICK TAYLER. 5s.

China Painting. By FLORENCE LEWIS. 5s.

Elementary Flower Painting. 3s.

Water-Colour Painting, A Course of. By R. P. LEITCH. *Eighth and Enlarged Edition.* 5s.

Flower Painting in Water Colours. By F. E. HULME, F.L.S. *First and Second Series.* 5s. each.

Tree Painting in Water Colours. By W. H. J. BOOT. 5s.

Painting in Neutral Tint, A Course of. By R. P. LEITCH. 5s.

Figure Painting in Water Colours. By BLANCHE MACARTHUR and JENNIE MOORE. 7s. 6d.

Sketching from Nature in Water Colours. By AARON PENLEY. 15s.

Landscape Painting in Oils, A Course of Lessons in. By A. F. GRACE. *Cheap Edition.* 25s.

A Primer of Sculpture. By E. ROSCOE MULLINS. With Illustrations. Cloth gilt, 2s. 6d.

Oil Painting, A Manual of. By the Hon. JOHN COLLIER. (Non-Illustrated.) 2s. 6d.

*** *A Catalogue of the above sent post free on application.*

CASSELL & COMPANY, LIMITED, *Ludgate Hill, London.*

Crown 8vo, cloth, 5s. each.

THE FINE-ART LIBRARY.

Edited by JOHN C. L. SPARKES, Principal of the National Art Training School, South Kensington Museum. With about 100 **Illustrations** in each

Engraving: its Origin, Processes, and History. By LE VICOMTE HENRI DELABORDE. Translated by R. A. M. STEVENSON.

Tapestry, A Short History of, from the Earliest Times to the End of the 18th Century. By EUGÈNE MÜNTZ. Translated by Miss L. J. DAVIS.

Greek Archæology, A Manual of. By MAXIME COLLIGNON. Translated by Dr. J. H. WRIGHT.

The Flemish School of Painting. By Prof. A. J. WAUTERS. Translated by Mrs. HENRY ROSSEL.

The English School of Painting. By ERNEST CHESNEAU. Translated by LUCY N. ETHERINGTON. With an Introduction by Professor RUSKIN.

Artistic Anatomy. By Prof. MATHIAS DUVAL. Translated by F. E. FENTON.

The Dutch School of Painting. By HENRY HAVARD. Translated by G. POWELL.

The Education of the Artist. By ERNEST CHESNEAU. Translated by CLARA BELL. (Non-Illustrated.)

*** *A Prospectus post free on application.*

CASSELL & COMPANY, LIMITED, *Ludgate Hill, London.*

4

www.ingramcontent.com/pod-product-compliance
Lightning Source LLC
Chambersburg PA
CBHW031158050726
47495CB00019B/2474